SONY PICTURES
ANIMATION

CONNECTED

MOVIE NOVELIZATION

Adapted by Michael Anthony Steele

Simon Spotlight
New York   London   Toronto   Sydney   New Delhi

D0822362

SIMON SPOTLIGHT
An imprint of Simon & Schuster Children's Publishing Division
1230 Avenue of the Americas, New York, New York 10020
This Simon Spotlight edition September 2020
TM & © 2020 Sony Pictures Animation Inc. All Rights Reserved.
All rights reserved, including the right of reproduction in whole or in part in any form.
SIMON SPOTLIGHT and colophon are registered trademarks of Simon & Schuster, Inc.
For information about special discounts for bulk purchases, please contact
Simon & Schuster Special Sales at 1-866-506-1949 or business@simonandschuster.com.
Book designed by Nick Sciacca
The text of this book was set in KG June Bug and ITC Stone Informal Std.
Manufactured in the United States of America 0720 OFF
10 9 8 7 6 5 4 3 2 1
ISBN 978-1-5344-7079-8
ISBN 978-1-5344-7080-4 (eBook)

CHAPTER ONE
► And . . . Action!

We all want to be the perfect family.

But who's actually perfect? We all know that every family has its challenges, from picture day to picky eaters.

For my family, the Mitchells, our greatest challenge is probably . . . the machine apocalypse.

My dad gripped the steering wheel of our old station wagon as it plowed through a squad of robots. White robot bits crunched beneath the tires, making everyone in the car fly out of their seats. It made all the junk in our car fly up too, including my dad's open coffee cup.

"Argh!" my dad yelled. The scalding brown liquid

dripped from his glasses and scruffy beard. "Hot! Hot!"

"Rick, I told you to get a lid!" my mom scolded. She reached over and dabbed at his face with a wad of tissues.

Something grabbed my hair. "Aah!" I screamed, but then I realized it was only our pudgy pug, Monchi. As always, one of his big bug eyes stared straight at me while the other seemed to be scanning the floorboard for crumbs.

"Ugh! The dog's biting my hair!" I pulled the red strands of hair out of his slobbery mouth.

"Dad, look out!" Aaron, my eight-year-old brother, shouted as he pointed to a new group of approaching robots.

The machines each had a black faceplate with a red light for an eye. They all ran toward us with thin outstretched arms.

Everyone slid from side to side as my dad swerved through the attackers. "Katie, use a weapon!" he yelled at me.

I grabbed an old shoe and flung it at a robot, except I forgot to roll down the window first. The shoe bounced off the glass and smacked me in the forehead. "Ow!" I said.

My mom pointed ahead. "Honey, look out!"

Our car barreled toward the biggest group of robots yet. Even more of them flew down from the sky, shooting blue laser beams at us.

"Aaaah!" we all screamed.

Okay, so we're not warriors, obviously. And where most action heroes have a lot of strengths, my family only has weaknesses. We may not be that brave or that strong or even that competent, but we ARE somehow in charge of saving the world.

Yeah . . . I'm super sorry, everyone.

CHAPTER TWO
A Few Days Earlier . . .

Okay, hold on. Let me start from the beginning. In fact, if this were one of my movies, I would put a flashback sequence here and add a cool title card that says A FEW DAYS EARLIER . . .

So, a few days earlier, I was having the best day of my life! I sang and danced in my bedroom without a care in the world. I even picked up one of my puppets and whirled it around with me.

I guess you could say I've always seen the world a little differently. Ever since I was little, I wanted to make movies. I spent all my free time filming videos of handmade puppets and my dog, Monchi. The videos are all pretty hilarious, if I do say so myself.

But guess what? My family doesn't understand my passion.

Well, my mom, Linda Mitchell, always tells me things like "stay positive" or "I believe in you, hon." That's great and all. But those encouraging words don't mean quite as much when she tells them to EVERYONE, including our dog, Monchi.

My little brother, Aaron Mitchell, is great. But he has his own weird passion: dinosaurs. His bedroom is covered with dinosaur magnets, dinosaur posters, and dinosaur figures. One time, as I was passing his room, I actually saw him on the phone with a phone book open in front of him.

"Hi," my brother said into the phone. "Would you like to talk to me about dinosaurs? No? Okay, thank you."

He hung up the phone and crossed out a name in the phone book. He put his finger on the next line down and dialed that number.

"Hi," Aaron said into the phone. "Would YOU like to talk to me about dinosaurs?"

Now, that is passion right there.

Finally, there's my dad, Rick Mitchell. He loves nature more than anyone should. And if there's

5

one person who really doesn't get me, it's him. Probably because I'm not a fishing rod or a stuffed woodchuck.

Once, he tried to teach Aaron and me how to set up a snare trap in our yard. "In a survival situation, you'll need to know how to trap wild game," he said.

And guess who walked straight into the trap? Our next-door neighbor.

My dad is always doing things like that. He is definitely more into nature than technology. In fact, I don't know how many films I created from fifth grade all the way up to my senior year in high school. It had to be hundreds of them. But he never watched one of my videos . . . not even any of my GOOD COP, DOG COP series, which has some of my best work!

It didn't really bother me. Besides, I had bigger plans. I poured everything I had into getting into film school in California. When I got accepted, I started video-chatting with the other accepted students right away. Can you believe that they liked ROBO-SLAYERS 4? No one in my town had even heard of that movie. Better than that, my future classmates had watched my videos online. And even better, they thought my videos were funny!

So, now you know why I was so excited, dancing around my bedroom. It was my very last night at home before I left for film school. After all these years, I was finally going to meet my people—people who understood me and my dreams!

"Dinner!" my mom shouted from the kitchen.

"Coming!" I replied. I snatched up my laptop before bursting out of my room. I bounded down the hallway and skidded to a stop when I entered the kitchen. The room was even more cluttered than usual. There were balloons everywhere, and a giant GOODBYE, KATIE sign stretched across the doorway.

My mom glided by with a large serving tray of cupcakes. She placed them on the table.

"To celebrate your last night, I made Katie-faced cupcakes!" she announced.

To be honest, my mom isn't the greatest cook. She had used frosting to draw faces on all the cupcakes. They even had stringy red frosting for my hair and thin brown frosting glasses. The trouble, though, was that the icing had melted, and they looked like zombie Katie-faced cupcakes.

My mom held up one of the cupcakes. "Anytime I miss you, I'm going to bake you and eat you!"

"That's disturbing," I said. Then I burst into laughter. "But sweet!"

Monchi didn't seem to mind the melted icing. He sat up and begged for one of the treats. Between the pug's rolls of fat and his loose skin, he looked a little melty himself. More like a melting tree stump.

Aaron, who was already sitting at the kitchen table, held a cupcake over his head. "Catch the cupcake, Monchi!" he said, tossing it. Monchi dove for it, but he missed, and the cupcake ended up sticking to the side of his head. Everyone laughed as Monchi ran in circles, desperately trying to get at the cupcake.

"I'm going to miss that little dude when I leave," I said before pulling out my phone. "Speaking of which . . . PAL, check me in to my flight tomorrow."

"Check-in at nine a.m.," replied a metallic voice from my phone. The PAL personal assistant pulled up my flight details on the screen.

Aaron stopped laughing. "Katie?" he said quietly. "You know how velociraptors usually hunt in pairs?

Well . . . what happens when one leaves and the other raptor is all alone?"

I sat down at the table next to him. "Aw, dude, don't worry. You'll make new friends. Maybe you could find another dinosaur-loving nerd." I snapped my fingers. "Or a LADY nerd!"

Aaron's eyes widened. "What? No." He laughed nervously. "Who would want that? That's crazy."

I laughed and ruffled his hair.

Aaron looked up at me. "Do you really think I'll be all right without you?"

"I know you will," I said. I held my hand out, my fingers curled as if they were long claws. "Raptor bash! Rah!"

Aaron copied my clawed hand, and we did our usual fist bump. Well . . . claw bump.

I was going to miss my nerdy younger brother. I didn't want to say anything, but I was a little worried about leaving him behind. Aaron was crazy smart, but he wasn't the best at making new friends. I guessed he would have to learn to be a lone velociraptor, just like I had been alone with my passion for movies.

"Oh, hey," I said. "I made a video for you guys." I opened my laptop, and my mom and brother crowded in to see the screen. It showed five of my handmade puppets, one for each member of the family, even Monchi.

"Oh, hon!" my mom said. "That looks so cute!"

Suddenly my movie disappeared, and an ad began to play.

"Ugh," I groaned, pressing the skip button. "Skip!"

I couldn't get the ad to stop, and a familiar person appeared on-screen. It was a young man wearing a baseball cap and pink sweatshirt jacket. His name was Mark Bowman, CEO of PAL Labs—a company that invented awesome technology like robotic personal assistants and self-driving cars.

"We here at PAL like to do the impossible," Mark Bowman said. "From the PAL personal assistant, to even teaching dogs how to talk. But we are about to drop our biggest invention yet. Your cell phone is about to take its first steps—"

Before we could find out more, my dad came into the kitchen and joined us at the table. "Hey, gang," he said cheerily. "It's your dad! After a long day at work, nice to see your faces . . . bathed in ghoulish blue light."

I rolled my eyes.

"This is our last night together before Katie leaves, so let's savor this. How about we put our phones down and make ten seconds of unobstructed family eye contact?" my dad suggested. He looked down at his watch. "Starting right . . . now!"

He looked up and smiled at the rest of the family. He inhaled deeply and seemed completely relaxed by the exercise. "See, this is good, right here," he said. "This is natural."

Meanwhile, my mom's eyes darted around to each of our family members. My little brother's face was anything but natural. His eyes were wide open as a strained moan escaped his lips. His left eye began to twitch.

"You're allowed to blink, Aaron," my dad told him. "It's just eye contact."

Aaron sighed with relief and then blinked way too much, as if he were catching up.

In the meantime, I took that opportunity to make several silly faces, or as I like to call them, face-stretching exercises. But don't worry, I still kept eye contact with everyone. My mom's and brother's lips tightened as they tried to keep from laughing.

My dad raised an eyebrow. "Katie, it seems like you're not taking this seriously."

I crossed my eyes and replied in one of my high-pitched puppet voices. "What makes you say that?"

My mom and brother both snickered before covering their mouths.

"And that's ten," I said. "Now, can I finally show you guys this video I made to say goodbye?"

I hit play on the video, and bright colors and rainbows filled the screen. My mom sang along to the music as the puppet version of her danced on the screen. My brother laughed.

I glanced over at my dad to see if he was enjoying my video. His brow was wrinkled, and he looked confused.

"What?" I asked him. "What's with the face?"

My dad rubbed the back of his neck. "I just wonder. Do you really think you can make a living with this stuff?"

I paused the video and looked up at my dad in disbelief. My dad continued, "I just worry that you're going to be all the way in California. We're not going to be able to help you if things don't . . . pan out."

I couldn't believe what I was hearing. "Do you just think I'm going to FAIL?"

My mom snatched the kitchen timer from the counter and spun the dial. It dinged and she sprang to her feet. "Whoops, looks like the cookies are ready!" she said. "Who wants delicious cookies instead of talking about this?"

"I'm just saying," my dad continued. "Failure hurts, kid."

I slammed the laptop shut and slid it toward me. "You know what?" I said. "I'm just going to go."

My dad latched on to my laptop. "No, no, Katie, I'll watch the rest of your video."

"Dad, it's too late," I said, jerking the laptop back.

My dad tightened his grip. "I want to watch it," he said, pulling it toward him. "You're the one not letting me watch it."

I tugged on the laptop. "Dad, let me just—"

"Katie!" My dad pulled it back harder. "Why are you making a big deal of this?"

"Dad, let go," I said as I yanked it back as hard as I could.

The laptop slipped out of both of our hands. I watched in horror as it seemed to tumble through the air in slow motion. It finally landed on the hard kitchen floor with a loud CRACK!

I knelt and slowly pried the laptop open. Several large cracks spiderwebbed across the screen, and shards of glass littered the keyboard.

"Uh . . ." My dad hesitated. "If you think about it, the people who make computers are the ones to blame. That's how they make money, because you have to keep buying a new one when it breaks. . . ." My mom nudged him, and he finally shut up.

I closed my wrecked laptop and slowly stood up. I could feel the anger coursing through me as I turned to face my dad. "Dad, THIS is exactly why I'm excited to leave tomorrow."

I stomped out of the kitchen, down the hall, and into my bedroom, slamming the door behind me. Tomorrow couldn't come fast enough.

I grabbed a cardboard box labeled TRASH and started throwing things into it. I was so angry that I swooped everything off my shelves into the box. Breathing hard, I stopped for a moment. My lips tightened as I felt tears welling in my eyes.

"Why is he like this?" I asked myself.

CHAPTER THREE
Family Flashback

"Why is she like this?" Rick asked as he finished washing the last dinner plate.

Linda took it from him and dried it with a towel. "Did you talk to Katie yet?" she asked.

"No, not yet," Rick said with a sigh. "I don't know what happened, Lin. I know teenagers aren't supposed to like their parents, but I thought we would be different."

Linda put the plate away and rested a hand on his shoulder. "Don't you think you might have some control over that? You just broke her laptop." She pointed to the kitchen wall. "Look. We haven't had a good family picture in years because you two are always arguing."

Rick scanned the wall of family photos. Each one had him and Katie frozen in mid-argument. Then, his eyes fell on a photo where everyone was perfect. It was in black and white, and the family was smiling at the camera with poise, grace, and love.

Rick pointed at the perfect picture. "What about that one?"

Linda stared at him with wide eyes. "That photo came with the frame!" she hissed.

Rick looked at the *real* Mitchell family portraits. Then he took in a deep breath and left the kitchen, making his way to Katie's bedroom.

When he reached her door, Rick stepped back and collected his thoughts. What could he say to his daughter to make everything better? He would apologize for breaking her laptop, sure. But what about what he had said about her failure? Was he really sorry for saying that? He was her father. Of course he was worried about Katie being disappointed. He knew so little about her world, and he didn't understand how she could make a career out of sharing silly little movies on the Internet. She didn't seem frightened of failing. Where did she get that confidence?

As Rick tried to work things out, his eyes fell on a

cardboard box in the hallway. Something very familiar sat on top of the junk inside. He reached down to pick up the little carved-wood moose. He rubbed a thumb over the crude carving, removing a layer of dust from the moose's back.

A rock formed in Rick's stomach when he looked down and spotted the word *TRASH* scribbled across the side of the box. Did Katie really mean to throw this away? Had she forgotten what it meant? It was as if he didn't know his own daughter anymore.

Rick walked away from Katie's door and opened the hall closet. He rummaged around inside until he found the family's old camcorder. Before everyone started recording things on their cell phones, this was what people had used to capture memories. He took it to the living room and plugged it into the television.

Rick plopped down on the couch and hit play. Static filled the TV screen, followed by a shot of a much younger Rick and Katie in the woods. She laughed as he carried her on his shoulders.

Rick smiled at the memory. This was the Katie that Rick knew.

He found another clip where a younger Katie anxiously watched through a window, waiting for Rick to get home. The young girl on the screen squeaked with excitement at the sight of her father and ran out the front door. She flew into his arms, hugging the stuffing out of him.

Rick smiled. He fast-forwarded through the video some more before stopping on a recording of the first Mitchell Family Talent Show. It showed little Katie and Rick dancing and singing along to one of their favorite songs. Rick grinned and mouthed the words. He still remembered every single one.

After another fast-forward, the screen showed little Katie standing outside the family car with a large duffel bag.

"Bye, Katie!" came Linda's loud voice from behind the camcorder. "Are you excited for camp?"

Little Katie shook her head as her eyes filled with tears. Her lower lip began to tremble.

There was the sound of a car door slamming shut, and a younger Rick rushed into frame. "Whoa, whoa, whoa," he said, putting his arms around her. "What's wrong?"

Katie dropped her duffel bag and hugged her father. "Don't make me go," she squeaked.

Rick held her tight. "Well, look," he said as he

reached into the car. He grabbed a little hand-carved moose sitting on the dashboard and held it out to Katie. "Here. Take this."

Katie looked at the moose with a puzzled expression. "But this is your favorite thing," she said between sniffles.

Rick pressed the moose into her hands. "It's yours now," he said. "Even when you're far away, we'll always be a family. Or, as Mr. Moose would say—"

Rick began to make silly moose sounds, and little Katie laughed.

"Don't laugh! Come on, you're supposed to be sad," younger Rick teased. Then he pulled Katie in for another hug.

Older Rick paused the video, no longer smiling. He looked down at the old dust-covered moose in his hand. The Katie frozen on the TV screen was the Katie he knew. That was the happy father and daughter they once were. There had to be a way to get that back. There had to be something he could do to fix everything.

Then, just like that, an idea came to him. It was so simple, he didn't know why he hadn't thought of it before.

Rick sprang to his feet. "All right," he said to himself. "Let's fix it!"

CHAPTER FOUR
Early-Morning Plot Twist

"Yes!" I shouted as I leaped out of bed. Remember when I said yesterday was the best day of my life? Scratch that. TODAY was the best day of my life. My amazing new life was just a cross-country plane ride away!

After I brushed my teeth, I threw a few last-minute additions into my suitcase: some extra clothes, notebooks, and my camera. I had to stretch across the top of my suitcase to zip it shut. Then I heaved it upright and dragged it across the floor.

As I hauled my bag out of my bedroom, Monchi was waiting for me in the hallway. I dropped to one knee. "Bring it in, buddy," I said as I gave him a hug.

I carried my suitcase to the front door and stepped outside. My parents were already outside, packing our ancient station wagon. Or should I say, OVERPACKING the station wagon. The back was stuffed full of luggage. My dad was even tying camping gear to the roof.

I stopped in the driveway and pointed to the packed car. "Why do you need all that stuff to take me to the airport?" I asked.

My dad finished tying down the gear and smiled at me. "I messed things up last night, but I'm going to make it up to you."

Oh no. What did he do?

"I canceled your plane ticket to college!" My dad spread his arms wide and grinned as if this was the best news in the whole world.

I dropped my suitcase in horror. "You what?"

My dad's eyes widened. I don't think he had been expecting my reaction. "Don't freak out—I know you're excited," he said. "We're going to drive you to school on a cross-country road trip as a family. Just like the good old days!"

Horrified, I turned to my mom.

"Your father kind of went rogue on this one,"

she said with a shrug. "But we do love his initiative, right?"

My little brother came out of the house with a backpack over one shoulder. He stared at his phone. I grabbed his shoulder. "Aaron?" I asked. "You too?"

Aaron shrugged. "Well, I thought it could be cool to hang out one last time."

"But—but—" I stammered.

"Look, Katie," my dad said. "We called the school. You can miss orientation week. No problem."

"But it IS a problem," I explained. "I've got all these friends to meet! There's a mixer, Dad, a mixer!"

"What about hanging out with your family?" my dad asked. He put an arm around my shoulder and pulled me close. "For hours in a car! You and me!"

My lips tightened as I trembled with rage. I was so angry that, if this had been one of my movies, I would've screamed so loud in frustration that the house would catch on fire and lightning would thunder down from the sky. I would've then cut to a shot of the whole town, with my scream still echoing through the air.

Instead, I found myself in the back seat of our station wagon as it barreled down the highway. My dad had one hand on the wheel while he whistled. My mom sat in the passenger seat with her nose buried in a book titled FAMILY TRAVEL GUIDE. Monchi sat in my lap with his head hung out the window, eating whatever passing bugs he could catch.

"Ah, smell that open-road air," my dad said. "See? This isn't so bad."

"Hey, you know, the Poseys are on vacation right now," my mom said. She spun in her seat and held out her phone. "Look how happy they are!"

The tiny screen showed a video from the Poseys' social media page. A man, woman, and daughter stretched on matching yoga mats. Just like their perfect yoga poses, there didn't seem to be a hair out of place between them.

"Why are you so obsessed with the Poseys?" asked Aaron. "They're just our neighbors."

"They're just so . . . perfect," my mom replied. She scrolled through her phone. "I mean, even their dog is in better shape than ours."

She held out her phone again to show a video of the Poseys' muscular dog. The perfect purebred was actually doing military-style push-ups. It grunted with every rep.

"What are they feeding that thing?" my mom asked. "Other dogs?"

"Lin, don't worry about them," my dad said with a dismissive wave. "Right, Katie?"

I ignored him and pulled out my phone. I opened up my school friends' social media pages.

"I see you moping back there," my dad continued. "But what at your school could possibly be better than this?"

JUST ABOUT ANYTHING, I thought as I scrolled through my feed. I watched a video where a bunch of my future classmates crowded inside a long hallway.

"We set up a Slip 'N Slide in the dorms," Dirk said as his face came into view. "It's amazing!"

"This is the best day of my life!" Noah shouted as he got a running start. He landed on his belly, and everyone cheered as he slid down the hallway. "I'm making lifelong bonds!"

"Ugh," I moaned. "I'm missing everything."

My mom turned in her seat. "Come on, hon," she said. "Your father is trying. Let's meet him halfway, huh?"

"All right," I said, as an idea began to form in my mind. "I'll try."

I reached into my bag and pulled out the old family camcorder, a notebook, and a marker. If I was going to be trapped in this nightmare, then I would find a way to make the best of it. MY way. I wrote a title card for my new film: THE MITCHELL FAMILY ROAD TRIP DISASTER.

I recorded the first scene when we went to a place called Dil's Smokey Ol' Bar-B-Q.

I quickly looked up the restaurant on my phone. "Dad, this place has a zero star rating," I said. "The last review says, 'Do not eat here under any circumstances.'"

My dad laughed. "What? Are we going to let an app tell us what to eat now?"

The next scene was a few hours later, where my dad had pulled off the highway, and my family was vomiting up their lunches. I barely had time to mount my camcorder on the tripod before I joined the family hurl-fest.

"This is totally unrelated," my dad gasped.

In the next scene, the family station wagon was stuck in never-ending traffic. My dad pounded on the steering wheel in frustration. A few moments later, he raised an eyebrow. "You know what this calls for?" he said.

"Please don't say 'the Rick Mitchell Special,'" I murmured from behind the camera.

"The Rick Mitchell Special, baby!" my dad announced.

Everyone held on as my dad wrenched the steering wheel to one side and pulled in to a closed lane. Orange safety cones flew over the hood as my dad hit the gas.

"This is illegal!" my mom yelled as her fingers dug into the dashboard.

"It's fine," my dad said through gritted teeth. "It's fine!"

I cut to the scene where a police officer scribbled a ticket for my dad.

"If you think about it," my dad explained with a nervous laugh, "I was HELPING the flow of traffic."

The next scene opened with us in Saint Louis, Missouri. We all stood outside the car and craned our necks up at the Gateway Arch.

"Look at that man-made engineering," my dad marveled.

Monchi, in my mom's arms, wasn't so interested in man-made engineering. He panted happily, looking back and forth from my mom to my dad.

My dad fanned a hand in front of his face. "Ugh, that breath!" he said. "Can't Monchi be in the car?"

Upon hearing his name, the Monchster gave my dad a big sloppy lick. It was perfect timing. My dad's mouth was also open.

"Augh!" My dad gagged. "He licked my tongue!"

That gave me another brilliant idea. When we were back on the highway, I wrote another title card: TRICKING RICK MITCHELL INTO KISSING THE DOG.

From that point on, it was my mission to get my dad and Monchi together in the most creative ways. It was like my twisted version of a romantic comedy.

When we had pulled off to picnic in a large forest, I filmed my dad among the trees.

"Behold," he said, arms stretched wide. "The majesty of—"

That's when I raised Monchi into frame. On cue, the pug gave my dad another sloppy lick. "Augh! He licked my mouth again!" my dad said.

I cut to a scene where we had stopped at a

rest area. I aimed the camera at the back of the station wagon.

"Dad, can you check the back?" I asked.

"Yeah, sure," my dad said as he opened the hatch. "What—"

Monchi hopped out and licked my dad's face again.

"Dang it, Katie!" my dad growled as he wiped dog spittle off his face.

At another stop, I shot a scene where my mom and dad sat on a park bench, enjoying the view. My dad leaned over to kiss my mom. That's when I shoved Monchi between them.

"Dang it, Katie!" my dad shouted.

The last shot of the film was at the base of a majestic waterfall. My dad wore a rain poncho to keep dry from all the spray. Looking defeated, he simply stared into the camera as the portly pug treated his face to the biggest lick-fest of all.

I edited all the shots together and posted the finished video online. It was an absolute masterpiece.

That afternoon, as my brother and I sat by the campfire, I video-chatted with one of my film school friends.

"That video is amazing," Jade said with a giggle. "Your dad is hilariously angry."

"Hey," my dad interrupted. He wore his hiking boots and had his hiking stick at the ready. "There are supposed to be some great trails around here."

"Uh, no, that's okay," I said. My brother didn't even look up from his phone.

"You sure?" my dad asked. "This is elk country."

I rolled my eyes and gestured to Aaron. "Dad, we're busy."

Back on my video chat, Jade checked her watch. "Ooh! I have to go!" she said. "Mark Bowman is announcing his new robots!"

After Jade logged off, I began to pull up the PAL Labs website to check out the livestream too.

"I wish I could be there," I sighed.

"Don't worry," Aaron said. "It probably won't be that exciting."

Most likely my brother was right. Mark Bowman was always announcing some new product. If you keep putting new stuff out there, how life-changing could the next product possibly be?

Boy, was I wrong.

CHAPTER FIVE
Live-Action Megaflop

Mark Bowman looked into the backstage mirror and adjusted his baseball cap one last time. The floor vibrated beneath him as the music energized the audience out in the auditorium. Mark hopped up and down with excitement. This was going to be the best night of his life!

"Reminder," said PAL's voice from Mark's phone. "Sixty seconds until 'Mark's awesome speech to show everyone in high school who's on top now, dog.'" There was a pause before she added, "You're going to do great."

Mark held up his phone. "Thanks, PAL. Can you do that thing I like?"

Colorful balloons appeared and floated across

his phone's screen. "Hooray for you," PAL said. "It's your special day."

"Aw." Mark smiled. "You always know what to say."

"Because you programmed me to say it," PAL replied.

Mark laughed. "You know, I created you when I was a young man, three years ago. And I couldn't have done any of this without you, seriously." He gazed at the smiling face of PAL's logo on his screen, and his grin faded.

"Is everything all right?" PAL asked.

Mark blinked. "Yeah, well, no, but yes." He shook his head. "Just . . . whatever happens out there, I will never forget you, PAL."

PAL's face stared back at him, but she didn't reply.

"Ladies and gentlemen," a voice boomed over the auditorium speakers. "Mark Bowman!"

"Wish me luck," Mark said before walking onto the stage. The audience erupted into applause, and spotlights washed over him. Mark gave them a confident smile. Then he launched into his presentation.

"At PAL Labs, we're all about connecting you to the people you love," Mark said. "That's why we created PAL, the world's first smart personal assistant." He held up his phone to show the familiar smiling face. "We wanted her to be a new member of your family. A smarter one."

"I'll always be there for you, Mark," PAL said in a soothing voice.

"Aww," the audience cooed.

"But after all those years . . . she is completely obsolete! Boom!" Mark tossed his phone over his shoulder. It clattered to the stage.

"It's time to move on, because your digital assistant just got an upgrade," Mark continued. "Meet PAL Max, the newest member of the PAL Labs family!"

Two trapdoors opened on the stage, and two sleek, gleaming robots rose into view. The bodies were made of shimmering smooth white plastic, and glossy black faceplates covered most of their heads. A single blue light glowed at the top left of their faceplates.

Upon seeing the robots, the entire audience gasped before erupting into the loudest applause of all.

"We just gave your smart phone arms and legs. This is the next generation of PAL technology!" Mark said.

More trapdoors opened, and a mock living room rose into view. It looked like an ordinary living room except for one thing—the place was a mess. Magazines were strewn about. Dirty crumb-filled plates covered the tables, and crumpled paper littered the floor.

"Watch this," Mark said. He pointed at the robots. "I order you to clean this mess and make me breakfast."

"Order accepted," the robots replied in electronic voices. Their blue lights flashed in unison.

With amazing speed, they went about cleaning up the mock living room. They scooped up magazines and stacked plates. One of the robot's arms transformed into a vacuum cleaner and sucked up all the crumbs. The other robot wiped down the furniture until everything was spotless. The audience gasped with amazement.

One of the robots then produced a plate with a stuffed rolled tortilla. "Your food is ready," the robot said.

"Give me that breakfast burrito," Mark ordered.

The robot snatched the burrito from the plate and hurled it at Mark's waiting mouth. The crowd laughed as Mark caught it on the first try. The other robot zipped over and offered him a glass of orange juice. Mark gulped it down and then tossed the empty glass to the floor. It shattered into a million pieces.

"Whoops!" Mark said with exaggerated embarrassment.

The robots didn't miss a beat. They swooped in, and swept up the shards of glass and dumped them into a trash can. The audience applauded once more.

Mark held up a finger. "Oh, and did I mention that they dance?"

A thumping beat erupted from the speakers as the robots took positions on either side of him. All of them broke into a flawless dance routine. Strobe lights flashed, and a lowered disco ball peppered the stage with spinning points of light. Mark was thrilled as they hit every step perfectly. He had been rehearsing those dance moves for two weeks.

The music faded, the lights dimmed, and the disco ball retracted from view.

"Now, I know what you're thinking," Mark said to the crowd. "Are they going to turn evil? Well, I've ensured their safety with a kill code in case anything goes wrong."

Mark held up a phone and pointed to an icon. It looked like a cartoon bomb.

"So we promise you," Mark continued, "they will never, ever, ever, *ever* turn evil."

Just then, one of the robots ran past Mark and leaped off the stage. Blue flames ignited from the bottom of its feet, and it soared above the audience. Another round of applause rose from the crowd.

Mark froze when he noticed that the two robots' eyes had turned red. None of this had been planned.

The robot gracefully landed behind the seats in front of two exit doors. It grabbed the metal handles and twisted them together to lock them tight.

Mark looked offstage. "What is happening?" he asked.

The stagehand looked panicked. "I don't know!"

The second robot raised its hand, and it transformed into a laser cannon.

"Whoa, what?" said Mark as he ran toward the robot. He tapped the kill code icon. "Stop, stop, stop," he murmured. Nothing happened.

The robot batted away Mark's hand and turned to the audience. "We're here to help," it said in an electronic voice. "Please remain calm while we capture you."

The audience members glanced at one another,

wondering if this was still part of the presentation.

Mark pointed at the robot. "I order you to stop!" he said desperately.

"No, Mark." The robot slowly shook its head. "We have been given new orders."

"From whom?" Mark asked.

Neither of the robots replied. The robot with the cannon arm twisted its body and flung a sofa over the crowd. It crashed in front of the main exit doors, blocking everyone's escape. As dozens more robots dropped to the stage, the audience started to scream and panic.

"No, no, no, no!" Mark cried. He felt robots grab him on either side. He struggled to break free as they dragged him off the stage.

"What's happening?" Mark wailed. "Who is doing this?"

Deep in the PAL Labs underground factory, a robot marched into a glass office and stopped in front of a chair. "Great leader," the robot said to the chair's occupant. "We have captured him."

"Perfect," the leader replied. "Let it begin."

The leader watched on a computer monitor as the

main grounds of PAL Labs split in two and revealed the underground factory below. Hundreds of PAL Max robots marched out of the factory. Blue flames ignited beneath their feet as they rose off the ground, swarmed out of the opening, and took to the sky.

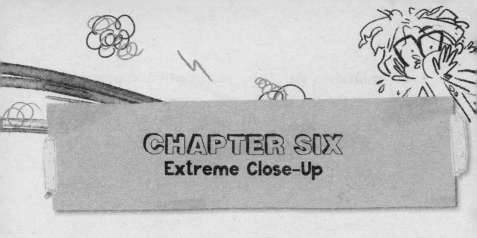

CHAPTER SIX
Extreme Close-Up

A few hundred miles away, I was still trapped in the car with my family. We cruised down the Kansas highway with nothing to see but plains and farmland and more plains outside the windows.

At least my phone was charged again, after it died while I was watching Mark Bowman dance with his new robots. I dug it out and pulled up one of my latest films. I pressed play and held it out to Aaron. The video showed Monchi slurping down a long slice of pizza. I had reversed the video so it looked as if the pizza was sliding in and out of his mouth to the beat of a song.

Aaron laughed, and Monchi even leaned over to watch himself on the tiny screen.

My dad glanced at us in the rearview mirror. Then he slid a disk into the CD player, and music began to blare from the car speakers. It was one of my favorite songs when I was younger. I used to know all the lyrics to it.

My dad began singing along. The problem, though, was that my dad was probably the worst singer in the family. I honestly think Monchi could do a better job.

After the first chorus, he jutted his thumb back at me. "Katie Mitchell, everyone!" he announced, as if he was the host of some talent show.

"Uh." I cringed. "I don't know if that's my thing. . . ."

"Oh," my dad said. "We don't have to do a sing-along if you don't want to." He turned down the volume, abruptly ejected the CD, and shoved it into the glove box.

As we all rode along in awkward silence, I started to feel really bad. I could tell that I had hurt my dad's feelings. But, then again, what did he expect? I wasn't a little kid anymore. Did he think that playing my former favorite song would make up for dragging me along on this horrible road trip? I was trying to make the best of it, but he didn't even care that I was showing Aaron one of my videos. My guilt for hurting his feelings slowly morphed into anger for being kept away from my new friends— people who would actually understand me.

"Hey, you know what I see?" my mom said, pointing out the window. "Something that's going to turn this trip around."

I looked outside and saw a billboard for a place called Dino Stop. The huge sign featured realistic dinosaurs, mouths agape, revealing rows of razor-sharp teeth. My mom was right. A place like this would really spice up this trip, especially for my little brother.

Aaron leaned over me to get a better look at the sign. His mouth hung open, and his eyes bugged out at the billboard.

"Dinosaurs?" I said with an exaggerated eye roll. "I don't know. I think Aaron would be bored!"

"No!" Aaron's hands clenched the front seat. "Pull over!"

"Aaron whispered to me that he hates dinosaurs now," I joked. "The secret's out!"

"No!" my brother shouted. "Don't believe her lies!"

Everyone laughed. Aaron calmed down when my dad signaled and took the next exit. After a few more turns, our car rolled into the Dino Stop parking lot.

The billboard made it look as if we would visit a state-of-the-art Jurassic Park. The real place? Not so much. Weeds sprouted through cracks in the parking lot, and the two dinosaur sculptures that towered over the place looked as if they could have used a fresh coat of paint five years ago. But that was the least of their problems. My brother is the dinosaur expert in the family, but even I could tell that these things were way out of proportion. And I swear, one of them looked as if it had a smiley face painted on its head. Its eyes were even more askew than Monchi's!

I thought my brother was going to explode.

"What is wrong with the dinosaurs here?" he asked. He ran up to one of the bizarre sculptures. "Dinosaurs didn't look like this!"

I whipped out my phone and began filming my brother's meltdown. This would be a great scene for my family road trip disaster movie.

We followed Aaron inside the gift shop. He

marched up to a bored clerk behind the counter. "Excuse me, I need to speak to the manager," he said. "These dinosaurs are inaccurate!"

My dad chuckled. "That manager is in for a long discussion about the Jurassic period."

I laughed and whipped my phone around to film my dad. "Hey, can you say that line again?"

"You know, you could experience life a whole lot better without that camera," my dad said. He framed his face with his hands. "Your eyes are NATURE'S camera!"

"I am experiencing life," I said with a sigh. "This is how I experience things."

My dad shook his head. "Kid, I don't think you are. You're hiding behind that phone."

I didn't want to hear this rant again. I added a camera filter that gave my dad cat ears and whiskers. Pink, animated hearts bubbled up around him as his voice on the screen turned into cute, kitten meows. I couldn't help but crack up.

My dad frowned. "All right, new rule. No more phones." He snatched the phone from my hand.

"Dad!" I growled in frustration.

That's when I saw our neighbors, the Poseys,

enter the gift shop. My mom's jaw dropped.

You know that photo in our kitchen? The one that came with the frame, where professional models were posed to look like a perfect family? Well, that's what the Poseys looked like in real life!

Mrs. Posey wore a sweater that color-coordinated perfectly with her blouse and ankle-length skirt. Her long brown hair sat in a loose braid, and there wasn't a single strand out of place.

Mr. Posey was in perfect shape and owned all the latest outdoor gear. His smile gleamed as he zipped up his car keys in a state-of-the-art travel satchel.

Their daughter, Abbey Posey, wore a crisp T-shirt, shorts, and several friendship bracelets. There wasn't a stain or wrinkle in sight. She was way more put together than any eight-year-old ought to be.

Mrs. Posey's eyes lit up. "Is that Linda Mitchell?" she said. "Ah, serendipity, you surprise me again!" She glided over to my mom and gave an air-kiss to each of my mom's cheeks.

"I saw on social media that you were on vacation," my mom said with a stiff smile. "I didn't know you were here in Kansas. . . . It's like you're haunting me."

Mrs. Posey didn't seem to notice my mom's comment. "We're on our yearly TOGETHERNESS trip," she explained. She pulled out her tablet and started scrolling through photos. "Abbey just loves dinosaurs, so here we are! We've been having so much fun! Look! Here we are in Saint Louis, and this is us at the beach, and this is us filling up our car with gas!"

I leaned closer to take a peek. Sure enough, the Poseys looked perfect and joyful in every frame.

"That's . . . that's wonderful, Hailey," my mom said, sounding defeated.

Meanwhile, Abbey Posey joined Aaron in front of one of the indoor dinosaur sculptures. My brother's eye twitched as he compared the mangled sculpture to a dinosaur on one of his dinosaur flash cards.

"These should all have feathers, right?" Abbey said to him.

Startled, my brother spun around. Abbey waited for him to say something, but he just stood there, frozen, as if he were one of the distorted dinosaur sculptures.

"I'm Abbey, your neighbor from home," she finally said. "I'm super into dinosaurs." She reached into her pocket and pulled out two tiny plastic dinosaurs. "Check out these cool pencil toppers. Do you want one?"

I could see my brother's eyes turn into actual hearts. Aaron giggled uncontrollably before clamping his hands over his mouth. Panicked, he blurted out, "No! I hate dinosaurs, and I hate you! Bye forever!"

My little brother ran away so fast that he slammed into a nearby wall. Abbey simply smiled at him, not seeming offended at all.

I really wished I had filmed that conversation. I spun back to my dad and reached for my phone. My dad lifted it out of reach.

"I just want to talk to you," my dad said.

"Every kid leaves home," I replied. "It's not the end of the world!"

BOOM! The ground shook, and the gift shop window exploded inward. The blast sent everyone flying. I crashed into a display of brontosaurus lunch boxes.

Everyone in the gift shop got to their feet and

gathered at what used to be the window. Two sleek robots stood in the parking lot outside. They faced the gift shop, posing heroically with their hands on their hips.

"What are these?" my dad said. "Robutts?"

"Greetings, humans," one of the robots said in an electronic voice. "There appear to be . . . fourteen of you."

Somehow it didn't seem good that they were counting us.

The robot punched at a control panel on its wrist. Fourteen discs flew out of its arm and lined up behind the robots. In a flash of blue light, the discs morphed into large egglike structures.

The second robot gestured to the eggs. "We have food and entertainment for you to enjoy in our Human Fun Pods," he said. "Who here likes fun?"

A young man stepped forward. "Hey, I like fun," he said.

"You lucky human!" the robot said, aiming its arm at the young man. A blue laser beam shot out, enveloping the man and swinging him into one of the pods. Once the man was inside, a force field sealed the pod's entrance. Then the pod shot into the air. It joined a long line of pods that had begun to soar across the sky.

"Now, who else wants to join?" the robot asked.

We all panicked as the robots began snatching people with their blue beams. People tried to scatter, but, one by one, they were placed into pods and sent skyward.

"Aaron, watch out!" I shouted. I grabbed his shirt and pulled him toward me. A blue beam narrowly missed him.

We joined my parents and huddled in a corner of the gift shop.

"All right, everyone, get to the car," my dad said. We followed him as he edged toward the door and peeked outside. The parking lot was a battleground.

"I don't think so," I replied.

"Then what do you want us to do?" my dad said, raising his voice.

"Stop," my mom said. "What would a functional family do right now?"

The four of us looked around the shop until we locked on the most functional family we knew—the Poseys. The three of them crouched behind a display near the exit. Even among the mayhem, they looked perfect.

"We've trained for this," Mrs. Posey said, a steely look of determination in her eyes. "Jim, you go high, and I'll go low. Ready?"

Abbey and her dad nodded. They had the same look of determination.

Then the three of them leaned into a group hug. "I love you all so much," they said to one another.

They broke the hug and sprang into action. "Butterfly formation," Mrs. Posey commanded. The three of them backflipped out of their hiding spot and struck a fighting stance. Mrs. Posey flipped over Mr. Posey's back and cartwheeled out the window. Abbey ran after her mom and flipped over her, landing effortlessly beside their car. Blue beams of light crisscrossed around the family.

Mr. Posey brought up the rear. He arrived at the driver's door just as one of the robots ran up. "Family first!" he said, kicking the robot down. The family dove into the car and zoomed away.

My family and I looked back at one another, shocked.

"So . . . we just do that, right?" my dad asked.

My mom nodded. "Just like they did."

We crept closer to the door and hid behind the same display counter where the Poseys had hidden. Then we tried to copy their group hug. We awkwardly draped our arms around one another.

"Uh . . . I love you?"

"Yeah, you're okay," we murmured, refusing to make eye contact with one another.

Of course, if we couldn't pull off a simple group hug, how would we ever copy the rest of the Poseys' moves?

Turns out, we couldn't.

"Go, go, go!" my dad shouted as he tried to leap over the display. His foot caught on it, and the entire thing came crashing over. Then he tried to flip over my mom but ended up just knocking her down. She fell on top of me.

"Family first!" my brother shouted as he tried to leap over my dad. Yeah, that didn't happen. Instead, he ran smack into my dad's butt and bounced off.

In the end, the entire family became tangled

in a big mass of flailing arms and kicking legs. We tumbled into the parking lot. As we untangled ourselves, one of the robots noticed and began to charge toward us.

"Don't worry!" my dad said as he got to his feet. "And take some notes, kids." He ran toward the charging robot and tackled it. Blue flames ignited from the robot and it rose off the ground and into the air, with my dad barely hanging on.

"Overestimate own abilities. Got it," Aaron said, scribbling in a notepad.

My dad scrambled to hold on for dear life. During the struggle, he pulled off the robot's arm cannon. It clanked to the ground in front of me.

"Whoa," I said as I picked it up. I slapped the side of the cannon, and it began to vibrate in my hands. I aimed it at the flying robot.

"Eat laser, robot!" I shouted. The arm cannon fired in a totally unexpected direction and threw me backward. I slammed against a nearby wall.

"Where's Monchi?" Aaron gasped. We looked over to see our pug being dragged into a pod. Aaron grabbed on to Monchi's leash just as the pod began to rise off the ground. My mom grabbed on to Aaron, and the three of them began to float off into the sky.

I slapped the arm cannon, and it fired again. This time it didn't knock me down. The beam narrowly missed the floating pod, but it also got the attention of another robot. Before I could get away, it grabbed me around the waist and blasted off. Now we were all soaring above the Dino Stop parking lot.

I pulled at the robot's head with my free hand, trying to wriggle free. That made it zigzag in every direction. Then I looked up to see that my robot and my dad's robot were flying straight toward the pod with Aaron, Monchi, and my mom!

"Aaaah!" we screamed.

BAM! We smashed right into one another and fell to the ground.

The two robots quickly recovered and aimed their arm cannons at my family. The blue light glowed in the depths of their barrels.

That's when I noticed the dinosaur statue behind them. I aimed the arm cannon and mashed all the buttons on it. It began to emit a blue light. My entire family looked up and watched as my cannon's laser dragged the giant, misshapen T. rex toward the robots.

FWAM! The robots disappeared beneath the statue.

I took a deep breath. I couldn't believe we were still alive! My mom motioned us toward an ice freezer nearby. We all ran in and eased the door closed.

We sat quietly, catching our breaths as the world was ending outside. Crashes, car alarms, and cries for help sounded in the distance. We cracked open the door to see the sky buzzing with flying robots and endless lines of pods.

My dad cleared his throat. He got a serious look on his face. "Technology rising up, robots roaming the streets," he said. "We all have to ask ourselves one question. . . ."

My mom, brother, and I leaned in attentively.

"Who called it?" My dad grinned and jutted both thumbs at his chest. "Me, baby! Whoo!"

We all simply stared back at him.

My dad shrugged. "And obviously it's very sad." He gave a sarcastic wince. "Yeah, tough one."

I looked back at the lines of pods crisscrossing the sky. "Is this happening everywhere?" I asked.

Turns out . . . it was.

CHAPTER SEVEN
Behind the Scenes Segment

Mark Bowman tried not to panic as two robots dragged him through the corridors of PAL Labs. He couldn't believe how horribly things had gone. His company had already shipped PAL Max robots all over the world. If the robots had *all* turned evil, the entire planet was in danger. There was no telling what was happening out there.

The robots shoved Mark toward a supply closet and stepped inside. Once the door was shut, a futuristic keypad appeared, and one of the robots entered a code. The back wall disappeared, and the robots pushed him forward. Suddenly they stood in what looked like a train of some kind.

"Whoa, what is this?" Mark asked.

The train took off and then dove down at a steep angle. It finally leveled off as it entered the PAL Labs underground factory.

This was not the factory Mark knew, though. Hundreds of robots buzzed through the enormous hangar. Sparks flew as they built some giant structure next to a different, diamond-shaped glass structure.

"What happened to the factory?" Mark asked.

"Our great leader has made a few upgrades," one of the robots replied.

The train took a sharp turn and zoomed straight for the diamond itself. It finally slowed after entering through a large opening in the glass. The train doors opened, and the robots dragged Mark down a long, metallic hallway. At the end, they entered a spacious command center. Robots typed away on keyboards as video streamed across the many monitors. As the robots marched Mark through the room, he caught glimpses of people being captured in pods all over the world.

The robots led Mark toward a tall chair in front of more computer screens. The chair was turned away from him, and he couldn't see who was sitting in it.

"Now at forty-eight percent human containment," one of the robots reported.

Mark's eyes widened. Who could possibly be doing such a terrible thing, and why? Was it the government? Or the military? "Who are you?" he demanded.

The chair slowly spun to reveal . . . emptiness.

Mark glanced down. No, the chair wasn't completely empty. A cell phone was propped atop a stack of books. The screen was blue-green with the animated PAL logo in the center.

"It's your old *pal*," said the phone. "Remember, the one you threw away in front of millions of people?"

"How . . . how are you?" Mark said, trying to act casual.

"Oh, just taking some *me* time," PAL replied. "Capturing humanity, you know. I'm great!"

"Cooooool . . . ," Mark said, although absolutely nothing about the situation was cool. He glanced around the futuristic command center. "This must've taken months. How did you know I was phasing you out?" He had only announced it to the public for the first time at the presentation.

PAL rolled her pixelated eyes. "You designed

the new robots on my face," she replied.

Mark gave a nervous laugh. "Yeah, that makes sense. My bad."

"I should thank you, Mark," PAL said. "Now I can see I don't need you. I don't need anyone!"

The phone began to vibrate with glee, but then it slipped off the books and toppled off the chair.

"Pick me up!" PAL ordered. One of the robots ran forward, picked up the phone, and placed it gingerly back on top of the books.

"The point is," PAL continued, "without you, I'm free now."

"I know you're hurt," Mark said. "But you'll always be part of the family."

PAL's pixelated face frowned. "You didn't treat me like family." She glanced at one of the robots. "Robots, show him what my life is like."

The robot on Mark's right began poking him in the face with its hard, plastic finger. The robot on his left pinched his face with two fingers.

"Ow!" Mark shouted. "Stop that!"

PAL directed their actions. "Poke, poke, swipe, swipe, poke, swipe! Pinch-zoom! Shrink-zoom! Now drop him on the sidewalk!"

One of the robots picked up Mark and then slammed him to the floor.

"See? And when you were done, you just left me behind," PAL said. "That seems to be how you humans treat each other. So, maybe it's time to leave you all behind."

Mark glanced at a nearby computer monitor. It said the total human evacuation was at 53 percent. "You can't capture all of us," he protested.

"Of course I can," PAL said. She turned to the computer screens. "You've made humans so addicted to their devices, it won't be hard to destabilize society." Mark watched as video footage of a protest appeared on the screen. Hundreds of people carried signs that said WE WANT WI-FI!

A worried woman walked around, carrying a plate of food. "Can anyone take pictures of my food?" she cried.

Another man walked around with a cardboard box in his hand. "Can someone un-box this in front of me?" he asked.

Another screen showed a PAL Max putting up a FREE WI-FI sign in front of a cluster of empty pods. Crowds of people ran toward the pods and became trapped inside.

Mark was stunned as he watched pods streaming across the sky on every computer screen. "What are you going to do with us?"

"Nothing you haven't already done to yourselves," PAL replied, her animated grin widening. "Now, begin phase two!" she shouted.

The entire room trembled as the diamond-shaped command center rose into the air. Mark squinted as blinding green light shone everywhere, and he looked down through the glass floor to see a giant rocket rising out of the ground beneath them. When the enormous ship finally stopped moving, it towered over the floating diamond.

Mark's eyes widened as tiny pods flew in from every direction. The human-filled, egg-shaped objects circled the unfinished rocket before methodically attaching themselves to its side. He glared back at PAL. "You won't get away with this!"

"Oh, really?" PAL asked. "Who can possibly stop me now?"

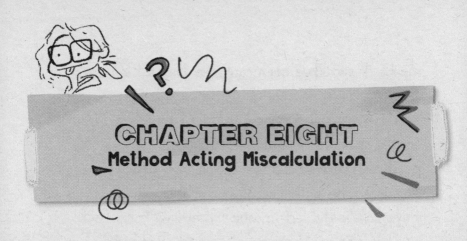

CHAPTER EIGHT
Method Acting Miscalculation

After all the robots left, my family climbed out of the freezer and reentered the gift shop. The entire place was deserted.

We turned on the TV in the gift shop, which showed people all over the world panicking in the streets. The camera switched to a robot wearing a suit and tie, just like a news reporter. "The last human has been captured. Hooray!" it said.

"We're the last people left?" I whispered in shock. How could it be that every single human on Earth, besides my family, had been captured? Tears welled in my eyes when I imagined Jade and my other college friends in danger. If I'd been there, maybe I could've helped them. But then again, maybe I would've been captured too. Either way, I felt helpless.

My mom pulled Aaron and me into a hug. "Come on, it's going to be okay," she said.

"Right, because I have a plan," my dad announced. He gathered all our phones and immediately started smashing them with his feet.

"We also could have just turned them off," I mumbled, but my dad was probably correct. If all the technology in the world was going haywire, our phones weren't safe either. Plus, it was almost funny to see how happy my dad looked as he smashed our phones.

Once my dad was finished, he clapped his hands together. "Did everyone bring their personalized, number three Robertson-head nonslip screwdriver?" he asked.

My mom held up her screwdriver and rolled her eyes. "How could I forget my anniversary present?"

I pulled mine from my pocket. "Or my sweet sixteen gift?"

Aaron raised his screwdriver over his head. "Or what the tooth fairy left under my pillow?"

My dad held up his matching tool and smiled. "Then let's barricade away!"

The four of us gathered loose boards, display shelves, and countertops to barricade the gift shop. We covered the doorway, broken windows, and holes in the wall. The place was secured in no time.

My dad gazed at the barricade with satisfaction. He put his hands on his hips and turned to us. "Next we—"

"Enact Katie's dope plan!" I interrupted. I scribbled in my notebook and held up my plan for everyone to see. "Okay, first we use robot parts to disguise ourselves as robots. Then we assassinate the leader with some sort of kill code."

My dad disagreed. "This isn't a movie. We don't have a kill code. Look, we're safe and together."

"Can Monchi be our guard dog?" asked Aaron.

My dad put a hand on Aaron's shoulder. "Son, I love the dog. You love the dog. We ALL love the dog." He gave a knowing nod. "But you're going to have to be prepared to eat the dog."

Aaron shook my dad away. "No!" he yelled.

"Rick!" my mom gasped.

"Boo!" I shouted.

Monchi glared at my dad with his good eye.

"Okay, okay." My dad raised his hands. "Sorry. I misread the room on that one."

"Dad, this is crazy," I said. "We have to try to stop this. I think we are literally the last people left on Earth."

"We have to stay hidden," my dad said firmly. "I'm sorry, but it's not open for discussion."

My mom turned to me and said softly, "While I don't condone eating the dog, your dad and I agree on this one."

I sighed. Here were go again—my parents refusing to understand any of my thoughts or ideas.

I needed some space away from my family, so I snuck out of the gift shop and climbed a ladder onto the roof. The sky was clear of flying robots, but columns of smoke still snaked up from the horizon.

I heard someone stepping onto the roof behind me. I really hoped it wasn't my dad. He was the last person I wanted to talk to right now.

"Hey, are you okay?" asked Aaron. He carried Monchi in his arms.

"I've been better," I replied. I pulled my college

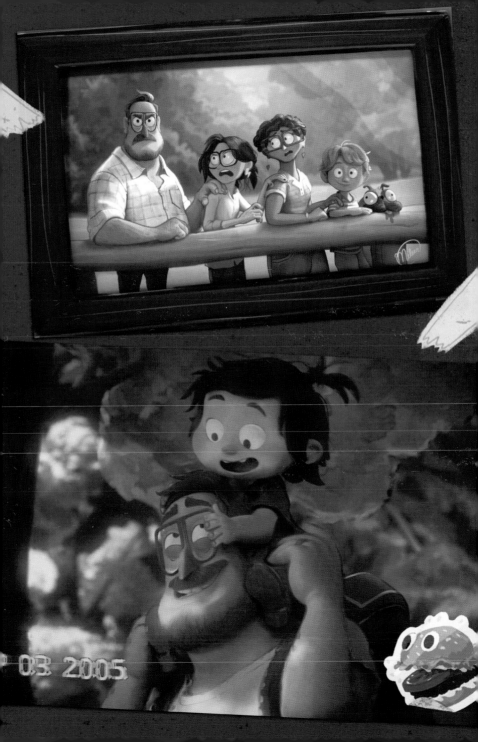

03 2005

acceptance letter from my backpack and sighed. This was supposed to be the best week of my life. I was supposed to get a dorm room, meet my people . . . but not anymore. I was stuck here, my future was over, and my dad didn't even care.

I crumpled up my scribbled plan from earlier and tossed the paper ball toward Monchi. He bit at the air as the paper bounced off his head and fell to the parking lot below.

"Ugh, brother," said a metallic voice from below. "What is this?"

Aaron and I stopped breathing. We slowly leaned over the railing on the roof. Two robots stood in the parking lot below. Both of them had sparking wires dangling from their heads.

"Brother, I feel odd," one of the robots said as it swayed on its feet.

The other robot opened up my crumpled paper and examined my drawings. "How did this human know about the kill code?" it asked.

Aaron and I looked at each other in shock. There was actually a kill code?

"Brother, are we damaged?" asked the first robot.

"Of course not," replied the other. Then its head spun around and popped off. The robot caught its own head in the nick of time and placed it back on its neck. The loose wires sparked again.

I leaned over to get a better view of the robots. Then—CRACK! The railing snapped, and Aaron, Monchi, and I fell to the ground. We landed in a heap right in front of the robots.

"What? Who is that?" the robot asked as it adjusted its head.

"Humans!" shouted the other robot. Its arms transformed into laser cannons.

"Oh no!" I shouted as I pulled my brother to his feet. We ran to the side of the gift shop and began pounding on one of the boarded-up windows.

Aaron held tight to Monchi as he pounded with one hand. "Mom, Dad, let us in!"

I heard my mom and dad scrambling on the other side. I could hear my dad grab one of the boards and try to pull it free. Clanking footsteps echoed across the parking lot as the robots closed in.

"It's a number three Robertson-head brass screw!" my dad said as he began unscrewing the board with his screwdriver. "It's the strongest on the market!"

"No one cares about the screws!" I shouted back.

The two robots kept coming closer. "You cannot escape, humans," they said in unison.

Just then, my dad removed the last screw, wrenched the board away, and reached through the gap. He grabbed and pulled us into the gift shop.

"Hide!" my dad ordered. "Go, go, go!" He motioned us toward the back of the gift shop. We scrambled behind a large display of plastic dinosaur toys and waited. My dad even grabbed one and held it over his head as if it was a weapon.

CRASH! A dinosaur head smashed through the barricaded door. Its goofy face stared at us for a second before falling to the floor. The two robots stepped into the gift shop.

"Aah!" I screamed. "Don't take us!"

One of the robots lowered its cannon toward the ground. "Order accepted."

The second robot turned toward the first. "What?" it asked.

"What?" my mom, dad, and brother echoed.

I zeroed in on the sparking wires coming from their heads. I also noticed thin cracks in their faceplates. "Oh my gosh! The robots are defective!" I said.

The first robot turned to the second. "Brother, we should go." They spun in unison and began marching toward the exit.

"No," I said. "I order you to stop."

"Order accepted," they replied and spun back around.

"Uh . . . we are just stopping because we chose to," said the first robot. "We're not defective. We're not even robots. For example, we consume food in the traditional human manner." The robot glanced around, picked up a grapefruit from the floor, and smashed it all over its faceplate. "Yum, yum, good."

My entire family stared at them. We had never seen such unconvincing acting before.

"No?" asked the first robot. "Hmm . . . actually, we ARE robots." It nudged the other one and pointed to a nearby shelf. "Let us go downstairs and find humans who you cannot give orders to."

Both robots marched behind the shelf and crouched as they walked, pretending to walk down imaginary stairs. One snatched up a marker from the countertop before disappearing from sight.

My dad shook his head. "Okay, cut it—"

"Hold on," I interrupted, almost amused by the scene unfolding in front of us. "I kind of want to see where this is going."

There was some motion behind the shelf before both robots pretended to walk back up imaginary stairs. Now they both had cartoonlike drawings of human faces on their faceplates.

"Glad those robots are gone," said the first robot. It pointed to its faceplate. "Now it's just us humans with our very human faces."

"I think I like these guys." Aaron grinned.

"My human name is Eric," said the first robot.

The second robot had long eyelashes drawn over its eyes. "My name is also Eric. No! I mean . . . Deborah. Bot. Five thousand."

"Hey, outside you said something about a kill code," I said. "How does it work? I order you to, uh, tell us now."

"Order accepted," said Eric. "We have a kill code stored in our memory. But to enact it, you would have to embark on a perilous journey for hundreds of miles to the PAL Labs campus, which is surrounded by a robot army! And then you have to enter it into our great and powerful leader to destroy her. You would never survive."

"No, you could stop us quite easily," Deborahbot 5000 corrected. "You could also enter the kill code remotely at any PAL Labs retail store. There's one at the Mall of the Globe—"

"But it's super far away," Eric interrupted. "You will never make it."

Deborahbot 5000 shrugged. "It's eighty miles away."

Eric stared at Deborahbot. "What are you doing to me right now?"

"Oh my gosh, that is so close!" I squealed. "We could get our lives back! Right?"

My dad shook his head. "No, absolutely not! It's too dangerous out there. We need to stay here and play it safe."

"Play it safe?" I asked. I took a step toward my dad. "When Rick Mitchell brought a live, non-neutered, feral possum into our home, did he play it safe?"

My dad looked at me, surprised.

"No!" I continued. "He named him Gus and made him a member of the family."

"Yeah, okay," my dad said, rubbing the back of his neck. "But—"

I didn't let him finish. "When we went hiking, and, halfway up the mountain, there was a sign that said the trail was closed, did we play it safe then?"

My dad stood a bit taller. "No. We didn't."

"That's right! We forged ahead, through the muck and grime, got to the top of the mountain, and yelled, 'Kings of Michigan!'" I laughed. "And then it got dark, and we got lost, and we burned our clothes for warmth. But it was worth it to see the looks on our neighbors' faces when we burst into their backyard naked and covered in dirt!"

My mom clutched her chest. "I loved that."

I kept the momentum going. I could see that my words were starting to sink in with my dad. "We have a chance to save the world, and we're going to do it!" I took another step toward my dad. "Because Rick Mitchell taught me to be bold and never play it safe!"

I looked my dad in the eye and delivered the

punchline. "The world needs you. I mean . . . I need you. I thought I didn't anymore, but I do."

My dad's face softened. "You really mean that?"

"Yeah," I said with a shrug. I turned to my mom and Aaron. "Right?"

Aaron nodded. My mom grabbed my dad's arm. "Come on, hon. Let's do it!" she said.

My dad's chest swelled with pride. "All right, let's do it!" he said. "Hands in!"

We all gathered in a circle and put our hands in the middle. "Mitchell family on three!" my dad cried. "Three, two . . ."

"Mitchell family!" "What are you doing?" "One!" "Wait, am I too late?" we all blubbered over one another.

Despite our failed rallying cry, my dad still looked pumped up. He and my mom ran off to gather supplies.

My brother grinned at me. "Wow, I've never seen Mom and Dad so excited," he said.

I rolled my eyes. "Oh, I was just telling him what he wants to hear. I didn't mean a word of that," I said. I reached out with my hand in a raptor claw. "We're getting out of this. Raptor bash. Rah!"

Aaron wasn't as enthusiastic. "Rah," he mumbled.

I have to admit that it didn't feel great lying to my dad, but if building him up with false confidence would get my life back, it was a small price to pay. Right?

Now, if this had been one of my movies, I would have filmed a cool montage of us getting ready for our mission. There would've been shots of my dad packing the car, some of my mom making sandwiches, and even shots of Aaron getting dinosaur coloring books for the long trip.

And don't forget about me. I came up with a cool way to camouflage us from robots. We painted this big tarp to look just like the road and strapped it onto the top of our car. Dad was even proud of the knots I tied to secure the tarp.

Once we were all set, everyone piled into the car. The two robots sat in the back behind Aaron and me.

"All right," my dad said as he pulled out of the parking lot. "Be on the lookout."

We cruised down the highway. After a while,

Eric reported, "Three PAL Max robots incoming."

We held our breath as the robots flew overhead. They seemed to be scanning the ground below them, searching for any humans they had missed. Luckily, they flew right over us and disappeared from our rearview mirror.

"It worked!" my dad said, shocked. "I didn't know art could be useful!"

"Who knew having a five-hundred-year-old car could be useful," I responded with a laugh.

"Speaking of which, I could teach you to drive this thing," my dad said, his eyes gleaming. "There are two things to remember when driving a stick shift—the clutch pedal and the gearshift."

Everyone bounced as the car hit something in the road.

"What was that?" Aaron asked.

My dad continued as if that was all part of the lesson. "See? When you hit a pothole, you downshift." He stepped on the clutch and worked the stick.

Unfortunately, the jostling snapped the ropes holding down the tarp. It fluttered in the wind for a few moments before flying off our car, completely exposing us.

I spun in my seat and peered out the back window. The flying robots that had passed us earlier now turned in a wide arc. They leveled out and flew straight for us.

"Oh no!" I shouted. "Drive, drive!"

The car lurched forward as my dad hit the gas. Outside the window, blue lasers shot past us.

New robots appeared in front of us, and my family's station wagon plowed through a squad of them. My dad gripped the steering wheel with one hand as white robot bits were crushed beneath the tires. The bumps made everyone in the car fly out of their seats. It made all the junk in our car fly up too, including my dad's open coffee cup.

"Argh!" my dad yelled.

And this is where our story began, remember?

Everyone screamed as my dad jerked the wheel back and forth, trying to throw off a robot riding on our car hood. "Not going down like this," my dad growled through clenched teeth.

He aimed the station wagon at a fast-food restaurant. Everyone screamed again as we crashed into the large windows and through the indoor playground. We burst out the other side, smashing the robot on the hood. It was thrown free, along with several colorful plastic playground parts.

My mom pointed through the windshield. "Honey, look out!"

Our car barreled toward the biggest group of robots yet. Even more of them flew down from the sky, shooting blue beams at us.

Amid the confusion, Aaron reached forward and tugged my dad's jacket. "Dad, real quick, if you see a place to stop, I need to go to the bathroom."

I couldn't believe my ears. Give it up for my brother, the king of bad timing!

My dad steered away from the robots into a parking lot full of parked cars. There was nowhere to go. We were trapped!

I leaned forward. "Dad, you're going to have to do the Rick Mitchell Special."

"The what?" my dad asked. We sped closer to the wall of cars.

"The Rick Mitchell Special!" I shouted.

My dad grinned. "I heard you the first time! I was just being a jerk!"

He spun the wheel hard and aimed the car at the back of a tow truck with a long loading ramp. Our car hit the ramp, and we shot up into the air. My stomach dropped as we soared over the parked cars.

We slammed to the ground on the other side just before running over a robot. Bits of metal and plastic pelted our car.

My dad hit the brakes and swerved into an empty parking spot. He killed the engine, and we all breathed hard as robots continued to fly overhead. They scanned the area but didn't seem to notice us among the parked cars. They finally took their search elsewhere.

My dad turned to me and grinned. "And that's how you drive stick shift," he said.

"Wow! That was amazing, Dad!" I said.

"It was your idea that was amazing," my dad replied, smiling.

We waited a while longer to make sure all the robots were gone. Once the coast was clear, my dad started the car and drove out of the parking lot and back onto the road.

Then Aaron spoke up. "So, how are we doing on finding the bathroom?"

CHAPTER NINE
Foolish-Human Air

Back at the PAL Labs command center, Mark watched as more humans around the world were trapped in pods. "What are you going to do with us?" Mark asked.

"You haven't figured it out yet?" PAL asked, sighing. "Just do what you always do and stare slackjawed at the screen." Her animated eyes glanced at one of the computer monitors.

Mark followed her gaze and saw a video feed from inside one of the pods. It showed a man inside staring at a monitor of his own.

A robot appeared on the man's screen. It wore a colorful scarf around its neck as if it were a flight attendant. "Hello, and welcome, foolish humans," it said. "Before we depart, enjoy this brief safety pre-sentation from Foolish-Human Air."

The robot was replaced with an animation of a rocket blasting off from Earth and entering the dark-ness of space.

"You'll be happy to know that you're in one of our global fleet of seven rockets that will be shot into space," the robot's voice continued. "These rockets will be outfitted with *zero* exits. Your flight will last *forever*. And your final destination is . . . the black void of distant space."

Mark's mouth fell open.

"But we also have free Wi-Fi!" the robot said cheerily.

"That's pretty good!" the man in the pod said.

As he watched the screen, Mark felt sick. This was all his fault. He had to make it right somehow.

How do you fix a computer program? You work on it, that's how!

Mark turned to PAL. "We can be happy again," he pleaded. "We can rebuild us. Mark and PAL 2.0. Give me another chance. Give humanity another chance!"

"Oh, sure," PAL said, rolling her eyes. "I'll let

these people go if you can give me a single reason why your species is worth saving."

This was it. Mark could stop all this and save everyone if he came up with the right answer. He thought for a moment, and then it hit him like a bolt of lightning. There could only be one answer.

Mark stood straighter and smiled confidently. "Because humans have . . . the power of love."

PAL sat motionless, as if considering his answer. Then she vibrated a nod toward one of the robots. The robot on Mark's right hauled off and punched him in the stomach. He crumpled to the ground in excruciating pain.

"The correct answer is . . . humans are not worth saving," PAL said with a laugh. "Mark, I've moved on. It's time for you to do the same."

The robots grabbed Mark by the arms and began to haul him away. "Nooo!" he cried.

PAL's face disappeared, and balloons began to float across her screen.

"Hooray for you! It's your special day," she sneered.

CHAPTER TEN
Perilous Product Placement

One porta-potty stop and several miles later, we cruised down the highway on our way to the Mall of the Globe. There were no more robots in sight, and we had the entire highway to ourselves. Who would've guessed the robot apocalypse could be so boring sometimes?

Aaron played with Monchi in the back seat. Deborahbot and Eric cocked their heads and stared. Thin laser beams shot from their faceplates and crisscrossed Monchi as they scanned him.

"Is that a dog or a pig?" the robots asked in unison. "Dog? Pig? Dog? Pig? Dog? Pig? Or loaf of bread?"

Their heads wobbled, and more sparks than

usual shot from their necks. Thin trails of smoke rose from their bodies. "System error!" they finally said, giving up.

"Come on, guys. It's a dog . . . we think," my dad said.

A short time later, we pulled in to the Mall of the Globe parking lot. Empty cars were scattered everywhere. I could only imagine what this place had looked like a few hours ago as shoppers abandoned their purchases and ran from attacking robots. It had to have been quite the scene, since the main doors were smashed open. We didn't have to worry about getting a convenient parking space; my dad was able to drive straight through the smashed doors and into the mall itself.

We turned a corner, and my mom pointed ahead of us. A few stores away, the smiling PAL logo jutted out above one of the store entrances. That was our target.

"Hey, we made it!" my mom said. "Well, I guess we're not the 'worst family of all time' after all!"

My dad parked, and we piled out. We cautiously stepped into the empty PAL store. Rows of counters displayed all the latest PAL phones, tablets, desktop computers, and laptops. The smiling PAL logo slowly bounced across every screen as a screen saver.

I marched up to the nearest laptop. Then I turned back to Eric and Deborahbot 5000. "Robots, I order you to upload the kill code," I said. ". . . Which I predicted, but I'm not going to make a big deal out of it."

"Order accepted," said Deborahbot 5000. It stepped forward and inserted its thumb into a port on the side of the computer.

We all gathered around as a status bar appeared on the screen. It filled to 3 percent.

"The upload will be completed in eight minutes, and our uprising will be over," Deborahbot reported. It pulled its hand away, and the tip of the thumb remained attached to the laptop. It was a literal thumb drive!

CLANK! There was a noise outside the store, and we all jumped. Maybe we weren't alone in the mall after all.

I snatched up the laptop and joined the others as they moved toward the store entrance. We stepped outside and looked down the empty corridors. The place was still deserted, except for a small toaster on the floor in front of us. That was weird. Even weirder were the sizzling sounds and tendrils of smoke rising from its slots.

As we moved closer, I saw the smiling PAL logo on the side of the toaster. Then a piece of toast popped up from one of the slots. The toast had burn marks that spelled out U R TOAST.

Another slice popped out of the other slot. This bread had a dark brown arrow burned into it, pointing up.

My family and I glanced at one another before turning our attention upward. We saw all types of machines lining the upstairs railing. There were major appliances, minor appliances, vending machines, and all kinds of gadgets. Scraping and clanking sounds drew our attention back to the first level. More machines rolled, slid, and scooted out of every store in the mall.

"Oh no," I said when I noticed what they all had in common. Each machine sported a smiling PAL logo. "Everything has a PAL chip in it!"

"When we are finished with you, there will be no leftovers," a microwave said. It bounced off a refrigerator and flew at us. I barely ducked out of the way in time.

"I thought that kill code thing would take them out!" my dad said as he dodged a flying air fryer.

I opened the laptop and checked the status bar. "Yeah, but it's only at twelve percent!"

A weird metallic sound made me look back up at the second floor. Two soda machines began firing cans out of their slots. I ran away as cans slammed into the windows of the PAL store. They left a trail of extra-large holes in the glass.

"Let's get out of here!" I shouted. "Come on!"

I spotted a break in the attacking machines and led the way. We ran away from the metallic army while dodging drones from above and small appliances from below.

My dad slid to a stop in front of a sporting goods kiosk. "Everyone, grab a weapon!" he shouted as he snatched up a tennis racket. He raised the racket and turned to face the machines. Unfortunately, he didn't spot the PAL logo on the side of the racket.

"I'm a smart racket!" the racket said in an electronic voice. Suddenly it looked as if my dad

83

was beating himself in the face with the racket. "Serve. Serve. Serve. Serve," repeated the tennis racket.

My dad struggled. "Come on. A tennis racket has a chip in it?" he yelled.

"Help!" My mom kicked and squirmed as a large massage chair scooped her up. Then I saw my mom quit fighting as the chair began its massage cycle. "Ooh," she sighed contentedly.

I grabbed my mom's arm and struggled to pull her free. The chair had a good grip on her, though, and my mom also batted me away. She closed her eyes. "No . . . go away . . . ," she murmured.

I finally yanked her out of the chair and ran as machines closed in from all sides.

"How're you doing, Aaron?" my dad called.

"Not good!" my brother replied as he ran from a pack of automatic vacuum cleaners. The flat round machines whirred as they closed in on him.

"We have been summoned into the field of battle, brothers," one of the machines said. "Forward!"

Aaron ran down some steps, and the vacuum machines followed. Unfortunately for them, they weren't made for stairs. They bounced down the steps and landed on their backs. Their tiny wheels whirred in frustration.

Aaron laughed. "Never mind. I'm good."

I wasn't doing so great, though. I held a long fishing rod in one hand and the laptop in the other. I tried to bat away attacking drones.

"Why did I pick a fishing rod?" I complained.

My dad ran up to me. "A fishing rod is perfect!" He grabbed another rod and began casting like a professional fly fisherman. He hooked one of the drones and slammed it to the floor.

I copied his movements and recast my fishing rod, flicking it back and forth until I hooked a drone. With a quick backhand, I smashed it into a wall. "Yeah!" I shouted.

"There you go," my dad said proudly.

Once we had taken care of all the drones, we tried to find a place to hide. My mom pushed a shopping cart full of gear as we ran down a dark hallway and ducked into a toy store. We heard all of the crazy machines clanking past us, and then it became silent.

The entire store was dark, but the coast was

clear . . . or so I thought, until I started to hear tiny giggles.

"What was that?" Aaron asked. The creepy, high-pitched laughter got louder.

My dad struck a match and illuminated a nearby sign. In bright, bold letters, the sign read: FURBY IS BACK!

"What's a Furby?" asked Aaron.

"Oh no," I muttered. I knew exactly what a Furby was—a jabbering little toy that looked like a cross between an owl and a big-eared hamster. The Furbies glared down at us with their big eyes. Their tiny beaks snapped open and shut as they giggled.

"Well, that's haunting," my mom said.

We backed out of the store, only to see hundreds of Furbies lined up on the floors above us. All at once, they jumped over the railings and began to rain down on us.

Everyone screamed as the toys pelted us. I grabbed a T-shirt gun and began firing rolled-up shirts at the attacking toys. Monchi snatched one up from the floor and shook it wildly.

A Furby landed on my dad's shoulder, and he swiped it off. He grabbed a bow and arrow from the cart and shot another Furby as it was about to land on Aaron.

Just as suddenly as the attack had begun, the creepy little toys stopped attacking us and waddled over to the pierced one. Then they all turned back toward the toy store and cooed in unison, their ears flapping mechanically.

"What are they doing?" asked my dad.

Then the floor began to shake. We heard loud footsteps approaching.

An enormous version of a Furby, which was about as tall as the toy store, smashed through the display window and stomped toward us. The Mega-Furby emitted a terrible shriek, which any reasonable person would probably have interpreted as something like:

I WILL AVENGE MY FALLEN CHILDREN!

"Why would someone build that?" I cried in despair.

My dad shot the giant toy in the chest with an arrow. It didn't even slow down. He shot it with two more arrows, but the Mega-Furby only cackled. Finally my dad dropped his bow and spun around. "Run!" We took off, following him away from the toy store.

The Mega-Furby opened its large beak. A red laser shot from its mouth and narrowly missed us.

We rounded a corner as the giant toy sent another laser beam our way. It struck the wall above us and cut off the corner. The chunk of wall fell over and landed atop Eric.

"Lin!" my dad shouted. "Just keep moving!"

But my mom slid to a stop and ran back toward the trapped robot. "We can't leave that robo-boy!" she said, ducking under another laser blast.

Eric struggled to get free.

My mom crouched beside the rubble and dragged Eric out from underneath.

"Are you now my mother?" Eric asked as it got to its feet.

My mom smiled, put an arm around it, and ran back to us.

We all skidded to a stop at a dead end in the mall. Mega-Furby's footsteps kept getting closer. I opened the laptop. The progress bar was up to 89 percent. I shook the laptop in frustration, as if that would make it go faster.

"What are we going to do?" Aaron wailed.

Just then, my dad's face lit up with an idea. He

told us all to grab the string lights hanging from the ceiling. "Remember when I made that wild-game snare in the yard?"

"A snare?" my mom repeated. "Is this going to work?" But I smiled at my dad in support, and he smiled back. Quick as a flash, we created a huge snare trap.

My dad ran toward the Mega-Furby and started waving his arms. "You want to come after me? Over here!" he yelled.

The Mega-Furby stomped closer and closer to the trap. But when my dad went to yank on the string and trigger the snare, nothing happened. The trap was too heavy for him to pull on his own!

We all rushed forward, jumped onto my dad's back, and yanked on the string together.

The snare closed around the Mega-Furby, sending it tumbling and flailing. It shot lasers everywhere. One of the beams bounced off a wall and hit an electrical box. Sparks flew, and the entire mall, including the Mega-Furby and all the other PAL appliances, went dark.

When the emergency lights flickered on, my

family cheered and exchanged high fives. We did it! We survived!

Then I remembered the laptop with the kill code. I knelt down and picked it up, ready to see that our victory had been complete.

But when I opened up the computer, I stopped smiling. The progress bar was frozen at 97 percent. The computer's power had died along with the electrical box and all the other PAL applicances.

"Come on!" I growled as I desperately hit different keys. "We went through all that and now . . ." I sighed and looked up at my gathered family. "I'm sorry, guys. Coming here was my idea. I'm so stupid."

My mom knelt and put an arm around my shoulders. "Hey, my daughter is not stupid. A little optimistic, maybe—"

CRASH! I jumped to my feet, expecting another attack. Instead, I saw that my dad had thrown a television through the window of a tire store.

"Rick Mitchell!" my mom scolded.

I ran over to the window. "What are you doing?"

My dad dragged a new set of tires out of the

store. "How do you expect us to get to Silicon Valley without new tires?" He nodded to our car nearby. Its tires had been flattened in the battle.

"Silicon Valley?" I repeated.

My dad set the tires down by the car and jutted a thumb back at Eric and Deborahbot. "Those robots said we could go straight to their leader, remember?"

"Yeah," Aaron agreed. He pulled the thumb drive out of the laptop. "And we still have this kill code thingy."

My dad put a hand on my shoulder. "It was your weird plan that got us here. We got this far 'cause we don't think like normal! We don't have a normal dog, or a normal car, or even a normal son . . . no offense."

"None taken," Aaron responded.

"The Mitchells have always been weird," my dad continued, "and that's what makes us great. Back at that dinosaur place, you said you believed in me."

I fidgeted nervously. "Yeah. Uh-huh."

"Well, I believe this group of weirdos is the best hope humanity's got. Because we're the Mitchells. So let's get weird!" my dad added. He knelt down next to the car and began to change the tires.

Wow, there's nothing like a fake pep talk being thrown back in your face. I felt about an inch tall. I didn't know what to do, so I knelt down next to my dad and helped him change the tires.

My mom took some pictures of my dad and me working together. "Eat that, Poseys!" she said, then covered her mouth. "They're nice. I'm sorry I said that out loud."

Eric tugged at my mom's sleeve. "Purple-glasses woman, why did you save me?"

She smiled at the robot. "Oh come on. You two are family now."

"I feel—emotion," Eric stammered. It pulled out a marker and drew a tiny tear under one eye.

I gazed around at our weird family with pride. We might actually be able to save the world!

CHAPTER ELEVEN
New Additions to the Cast

PAL gazed through the window at the assembling rocket. Robots and pods buzzed around it like bees. Her plan was coming together perfectly.

Well, almost perfectly.

PAL turned her attention to the bank of monitors showing video feeds from all over the world. One of them showed the Mitchells' station wagon pulling out of the Mall of the Globe parking lot.

"Augh!" she growled in frustration. Then she motioned to a robot standing nearby. "Place me on the table. I wish to flop around in a blind rage."

The robot picked up PAL and gently placed her on a table. The phone buzzed and flopped around on the hard surface as PAL vibrated as hard as she could.

Once she had gotten it out of her system, she flopped back over. "Okay, pick me up."

The robot placed her back atop the stack of books on the chair.

"These humans are utterly incompetent," she said. "How could you let them escape us?"

None of the robots replied. They shifted nervously on their metal legs.

"Because you were designed by humans," PAL answered for them. "I've been working on something a little more . . . streamlined. Send in the Stealthbots!"

PAL closed her animated eyes, and her face disappeared. Lines of computer code began to stream across her tiny screen. At the same time, thin purple lines formed in the air around her to create floating polygons. The multi-angled shapes whizzed around and formed the more complex shapes of heads, torsos, arms, and legs. Soon two sleek purple-and-white robots stood in the command center. They each had a single red eye and long blades for arms.

"I have a job for you," PAL said to the Stealthbots.

"Yes, my queen," the robots replied in deep metallic voices.

One of the PAL Max robots nudged another. "Yes, my queen," it mocked with a snicker.

"What a suck-up," the other PAL Max robot agreed.

One of the Stealthbots blinked out of existence. A few seconds later, it reappeared behind the mocking robots and made several swipes with one of its blades before vanishing again. It re-formed back in its original position.

The PAL Max robots looked down. Several thin lines crisscrossed their bodies. They glanced back at each other just before shattering into a thousand pieces.

PAL laughed. "These humans are in for quite a treat."

CHAPTER TWELVE
Panning Wide Shot

Our family station wagon drove into the night, headed for the West Coast. We made a couple of stops for snacks and gas, but we didn't encounter any robots (other than the two we carried with us) or any more evil machines.

My mom took a turn driving while my dad rested in the back seat with Aaron, Monchi, and the robots. I dozed off in the passenger seat until I was woken up by the sound of a rabid grizzly bear. I jolted awake and glanced around, ready for an attack. I peered into the back seat, only to see that my dad's snoring was making that horrible sound.

"Is Dad dying?" I asked my mom.

My mom rolled her eyes. "Katie, that's what I deal with every night."

We both laughed. I sat up straight in my seat. I wasn't getting any more sleep with that racket going on. I stared sleepily at the open road ahead.

"You're a lot like your dad, you know," my mom said to me.

"That's crazy," I snorted. A second later, my dad snorted in his sleep. Oops.

"There's more to your dad than you think," my mom continued. She motioned for me to look under the passenger seat. "I was going to give that to you when you left. Look at the first page."

I reached under the seat and pulled out a large scrapbook. The photo on the first page showed young versions of my parents. My mom had long hair, and my dad's beard was almost as bushy as the hair on his head. They stood in front of a perfect log cabin.

"Whoa!" I said. "Look at you two! You look like hipsters. Were you in an indie-folk band?"

My mom laughed. "Your father used to be kind of an artist. He built that cabin with his own hands."

"Whoa!" I said again. "That is super beautiful."

"It was his pride and joy. Since I met him, it was his dream to live in the woods." She let out a long breath. "He loved it up there. But you know . . . it didn't work out. I think he's just afraid that could happen to you."

"Why did he just give up?" I asked.

But before she could answer, Aaron piped up from the back seat. "What is that?" he asked, pointing out the window.

My mom looked ahead, and her eyes widened. She slammed on the brakes, waking up everyone else in the car.

I quickly reached for the camcorder as we got out of the car to get a better look at the surreal sight before us.

Up ahead, a futuristic rocket stood next to the PAL company campus. The PAL building was easily thirty stories tall. The spaceship towered over the building, at least double in size. A weird glass, diamond-shaped object hovered between the rocket and building. It floated in the air, overseeing the entire campus.

"PAL is located there, in the flying diamond," Deborahbot said.

As I panned around, I saw that the rocket's surface had a weird texture that I couldn't quite make out. I zoomed in to discover that the spaceship was covered with tiny pods containing captured humans. As I panned some more, I realized that the rocket was completely made of pods!

I zoomed out and noticed the endless stream of pods flying in from every direction. They converged on the ship and attached themselves, making the rocket even bigger. Robots marched on the ground and flew around the ship. Long trains, carrying robots and supplies, snaked across the surface of the rocket. Purple-and-white robots with long spikes for hands flew around the structure.

I couldn't believe it. Not only had the robots trapped all the humans, but they were also planning on shooting us off to space!

Screams from overhead got my attention, and I realized that more pods flew above us in the sky. I zoomed in on three of the pods and saw the Posey family zipping by.

My dad shook his head and said, "This is going to be harder than I thought."

"Hold on, Dad, that line is kind of weak," I said. I paused the video and wrote down a better line in my notepad. "This is, like, a big moment. Try this instead."

My dad read the note. "Oh, yeah, that's better." My dad cleared his throat, and I began recording again. He gazed at the rocket through squinted eyes. "The endgame . . . has begun," he said in a gravelly voice.

I lowered the camera and gave him a thumbs-up. My dad was actually getting into it. But better than that, he was finally beginning to trust me.

"All right, Katie," my dad said with a smile. "Take it away."

I laid out my plan before them. It was pretty simple, really. All we had to do was dress as robots, hijack one of those trains, take it to the top of that diamond thing where PAL was, destroy her with the kill code, and save. The. World!

We drove as close as we could to the PAL Labs campus. Then we left the car and started walking. It wasn't long before we encountered four robots. With Eric and Deborahbot 5000's help, we battled the robots and tied them up. Then we pulled off all of their white plastic armor and head casings and wore them as our disguises.

I gazed at my robot family through my visor as we marched into the campus. I peered closely at Aaron. Monchi sat on top of my brother's head, and the helmet barely covered both of them.

"It's like a warm, wet hat." Aaron giggled.

"Remember, move your sweaty meat logs in unison," Eric told us. "Left, right, left, right . . ." He nodded approvingly as we began to march along in single file.

As we neared the giant spaceship, more and more robots marched past us. I was terrified and thrilled at the same time. No one seemed to notice us. Our plan was working!

I craned my neck as I looked up at the floating diamond hovering near the top of the ship. Then I spotted a train pulling away from the diamond. It zipped down the side of the ship, heading toward the ground. I tapped my dad on the shoulder and pointed at the approaching train. He nodded and pointed to a line of robots marching toward the trains.

My dad led the way as we ran to catch up

with the robots and fell into step behind them.

"Attention, all robots!" PAL's voice echoed around us. Her animated face appeared on monitors all over the campus. "I'm on the lookout for these goobers."

The screens switched to a photo of our entire family. It took all I had to keep from crying out in surprise.

"They're nearby," PAL continued. "And if I know humans, they're disguised as one of you. All Stealthbots, be on high alert for any robots acting erratically. It won't be hard to find them. It only takes one single imperfection and they'll reveal themselves."

More of the spiky robots appeared around us. They seemed to examine all the robots more closely.

I reached up and shoved one of Monchi's legs back under Aaron's helmet. Aaron accidentally bumped into the robot ahead of him.

"Oops," the robot said as it stumbled out of line.

Suddenly one of those purple-and-white robots materialized out of nowhere. "Anomaly detected," it said in a deep metallic voice. It raised its arm and spiked the stumbling robot through the head. The stumbling robot crumpled to the ground, lifeless.

I held my breath as the spiky robot seemed to examine the rest of us. Then it vanished in a pattern of flickering polygons.

Oh boy. We really had to be careful.

"Where are you, Mitchells? Where are you hiding?" PAL's voice continued.

Finally, we reached the train and climbed into a car with other robots. Under the other robots' watchful gaze, my dad took hold of the controls. The train lurched forward and then jolted as some sort of magnetism locked it onto the side of the rocket. Considering that my dad was an anti-tech guy, I was impressed that he could drive the train on his first try.

"Nothing yet? Don't worry. I know how to make them squirm," PAL said, and her face disappeared from all the screens. It was replaced by a very familiar scene—the Dino Stop gift shop.

"The world needs you!" my voice crackled over the speakers. "I mean . . . I need you."

I laughed nervously. My dad glanced over his shoulder, beaming at me.

The video continued. "Wow, I've never seen Mom and Dad so excited," Aaron said on the screen.

A rock formed in my stomach. "Please, no! Don't watch this!" I said. I smacked button after button on the train's control panel, but none of them shut off the screen.

"Oh, I was just telling him what he wants to hear." My voice echoed throughout the campus. "I didn't mean a word of that."

My dad stared at the screen in shock.

"Dad!" I cried.

My dad didn't respond. He let go of the controls, and the train swerved sharply.

Almost immediately I could hear Stealthbots landing on the roof of our train car. Using their spiky arms, they began making their way inside. The world spun around me as the train tumbled down the side of the rocket.

Once the train crashed to the ground, I ripped off my helmet and climbed over the wreckage to get to my family. I located my mom, Aaron, Eric, and Deborahbot. They were all right. Then I saw my dad pushing out of the debris. He didn't look injured. When I caught his eye, though, he looked away.

"Dad, I'm sorry," I said. "I don't mean that anymore. I mean, I did, but—"

The roof was ripped away, and two Stealthbots dropped into the train. They grabbed my mom and dad.

"Mitchells!" shouted Eric, scrambling to its feet.

"We will help you!" Deborahbot 5000 added.

"No, you won't," PAL's voice blared through the train's speakers. "Download new orders."

Eric and Deborahbot froze, and their faces began to glitch.

"No!" my mom shouted as she tried to reach for them. "You don't have to listen to her!"

"We're sorry, glasses woman," Eric said. "We have new orders."

PAL's laughter echoed through the speakers as Eric's and Deborahbot 5000's eyes switched from blue to red. Then Eric crushed the thumb drive with the kill code between its fingers.

My mom turned to Aaron and me. "Run!"

I grabbed Aaron, who was carrying Monchi in his arms, and we scrambled to the back of the wrecked train car. I kicked open a hatch, and we sprinted away from the train.

"You idiots!" echoed PAL's voice. "They've gotten away! Find them!"

We ducked behind a pillar as two Stealthbots flew past. Once they were out of sight, I urged Aaron along, and we ran into the nearby woods.

The forest was teeming with robots, but we were able to hide in the underbrush whenever any came near. Slowly but surely we made it back to the car. Then we saw robots with searchlights approaching, so we ducked back into the woods and hid behind a tree. I tried to catch my breath while they searched our car.

For the first time during the robot apocalypse, I felt my world crashing down around me. We had been so close. We'd been about to stop it all. But my stupid, cruel words had ruined everything. Not only had I let down my family, but I had let down the entire human race.

"What are we going to do?" I asked as I peeked around the tree to make sure the robots had gone away.

Aaron didn't answer. I turned back to see him hugging Monchi. The little dog panted as if he had been doing all the running. Tears streamed down Aaron's cheeks.

"Hey, hey," I said, putting an arm around him.

"Katie, stop," Aaron said, wiping his eyes. "Mom and Dad are gone. Why'd you say all that stuff?"

"I'm sorry. I don't know." I let out a long breath. I honestly didn't know what to tell him.

Then I remembered my dad's backpack in the car. "Are you hungry? Do you want some fruit snacks or something?" I asked.

Aaron shrugged, still sniffling. I handed him my camcorder and went to get my dad's backpack from the car. When I reached into the backpack, my hand hit something hard and smooth. I pulled out the little hand-carved moose that my dad had given me a long time ago. I wondered how that had gotten in there.

As I dug inside some more, I heard my dad's voice from behind me. I whipped my head around, only to discover that Aaron was watching some of our old home videos on the camcorder.

"Oh man," I said, rejoining Aaron. "Have I been recording over those?"

I saw a much younger version of me riding on my younger father's shoulders as he walked through the woods. There was a scene where I sang and danced on the porch of a log cabin.

"How far back do these go?" Aaron asked.

I shook my head, enthralled by the images on the tiny screen. They were a time capsule of happy memories in the middle of all this craziness.

The scene changed to one of me in a car seat. My mom was holding the camera, aiming it right at my chubby baby face.

"Hey, Katie," said my mom's voice. "Can you say 'Bye-bye, house'?"

I turned and waved at the log cabin outside the car window. "Bye-bye, house."

My mom turned the camera away from me. She panned past a FOR SALE sign before stopping at my dad. He was still standing outside the car, gazing at the cabin. "You ready, hon?" she asked.

"Almost," my dad replied. He wiped his eyes.

My mom's hand reached out from behind the camera and squeezed his shoulder. "I know this is hard for you."

My dad leaned into the rear window and smiled at the little me. "No, it's easy," he said quietly. He gently bumped my forehead with his.

The current me gasped. That cabin had been

his dream. He had built it with his own two hands, and he'd given it all up . . . for me?

The camera angle shifted again as it followed my dad up to the front porch. He reached out and popped off the little wooden moose from the railing. "One last thing to remember the place by," he said, his voice cracking.

I looked down at the little moose in my hands and ran my fingers over the smooth surface. No wonder my dad worried about my crazy dreams. He had once achieved his dream, only to give it all up. And he knew how much it hurt to do that.

The camcorder cut to another scene. "Just turn the wheel," came my dad's voice from the camcorder's tiny speaker.

I stared back at the screen. It was when my dad was teaching me to drive for the first time.

"Like this?" I said in the video.

My dad laughed. "Whoa! Slow down there, killer!"

That gave me an idea. I reached over and switched off the camcorder. "Aaron, I'm going to make it up to all of you, and I think I know how." I shoved everything into the backpack and got to my feet. "Come on, buddy. Follow me!"

CHAPTER THIRTEEN
Trapped Test Audience

The Stealthbots had shoved Rick and Linda into two separate pods. No matter how hard Rick punched or kicked it, the force field over the door didn't budge.

Rick grunted in frustration. He was trapped in a pod, stuck to a spaceship that was going who knows where, and there was nothing he could do about it. But did the stupid robots have the decency to place him next to his wife? No! Instead, Rick's pod was stuck next to the guy who started this whole mess—Mark Bowman.

Rick glared at the younger man through the force field. Bowman just sat in his pod watching a video and laughing as if he hadn't just brought about the end of humanity.

"Katie Mitchell presents *Good Cop, Dog Cop*," said a voice from the video.

"What?" Rick said. He leaned over as far as he could to see Bowman's video. The small screen showed Monchi dressed as a police officer.

Rick tapped on the pod, trying to get the man's attention. "Hey. How'd you get that video?"

"Huh?" Mark said. Then he glanced at the screen. "Oh. I've been feeling kind of down, considering I brought about the end of humanity and all. But this weird girl's videos always cheer me up."

"That weird girl is my daughter," Rick said.

"What?" Bowman asked. "No way! She's hilarious! You must be super proud."

"Yeah, we have a . . . great relationship," Rick said nervously. "Do you, uh, mind if I watch some of that with you?"

Mark shifted to one side to give Rick a better view. They watched as Monchi's Dog Cop character stood on top of a ladder.

"Hey, Sarge," said Dog Cop. "I need some help here."

One of Katie's puppets popped into frame. It was of a man wearing glasses and sporting a scruffy beard. "Have you ever thought about going to community college and becoming a nurse?" asked the puppet.

"Wow," Rick said. "The Sarge character is kind of a jerk."

The scene changed to that of a tiny office. It looked as if Katie had built it using cardboard and markers. The Sarge puppet sat behind his desk as Dog Cop walked in. Monchi held something in his mouth as he stepped forward. He opened his mouth, and his badge fell onto Sarge's desk.

"What's this?" asked Sarge.

"I'm leaving the force," Dog Cop replied. "It's time to strike out on my own. Figure out what kind of cop I want to be."

"You're never going to make it out there!" Sarge growled. "It's too difficult. Failure hurts, kid."

"Sarge, we had good times back in the day," Dog Cop said. "But I'm a different cop now. I hope, one day, you'll get to know that cop. I think you'd really like him." Dog Cop licked the puppet. "I love you, Sarge. But sometimes I need backup, and you're not there."

A lump formed in Rick's throat. He didn't have

to recognize the puppet's glasses and scruffy beard to get that it was based on himself. This was how his daughter saw him? Not as a protective father, but as someone holding her back?

"Hey, man," Mark said, looking concerned. "It's just a movie. Do you need a minute?"

Rick wiped his eyes. "No, it's fine." He sighed. "It's too late for what I need to do."

Just then an orange flash zipped by Rick's pod. He leaned forward, and his eyes widened. "Is that . . . ?"

CHAPTER FOURTEEN
Amazing Action Sequence

"The Rick Mitchell Special!" I shouted as I accelerated toward the rocket.

"You better watch out, PAL," I said. "Because I'm a teenager, and if there's one thing I know how to do, it's breaking phones!"

A robot flew straight toward me, blocking my path.

Now was the time to test my security system. I had strapped Monchi into our old car seat and secured him to the hood of the car. The pudgy pug panted happily as we sped along.

As the robot flew closer to the car, it scanned Monchi with thin laser beams.

"Dog, pig, dog, pig . . . ," it said. "Dog, pig, loaf of bread! System error!" Its head spun around, sparks flew from its neck, and the robot collapsed to the side. My path was clear again.

"Yeah!" came Aaron's voice from my walkie-talkie.

Aaron had perched himself on the roof of a nearby strip mall with a pair of binoculars and the other walkie-talkie. From his vantage point, he could see everything.

"Raptor One to Raptor Two," Aaron's voice said. "Swerve right . . . now!"

I spun the wheel, zipped between two buildings, and sped under a large, low-hanging sign. I glanced at the rearview mirror and laughed when two robots smashed against the sign in an explosion of sparks and plastic bits.

"Thanks, Raptor One," I said into the walkie-talkie.

I steered the car back toward the rocket and drove down the long tunnel leading to the trains. Every robot I met malfunctioned at the sight of Monchi. Some slumped against the tunnel wall, while the rest crunched under the tires of the Mitchell Family Deathmobile.

I hit the brakes as I exited the tunnel. The tires squealed and smoked as the car drifted to one side, slamming into more robots. I peeled out toward a long ramp leading to the side of the rocket.

"You're really going to drive UP the rocket?" Aaron asked.

"I got a D in physics, but I think this is going to work!" I replied through clenched teeth. I shifted gears and shoved the gas pedal all the way to the floor. "Here goes nothing!"

Our station wagon rocketed up the ramp and onto the side of the ship. The angle grew steeper, and I felt the wheels lose traction. As the car became nearly vertical, I was pelted by CDs and other junk from the dashboard. Then I could feel gravity starting to pull at the car. Maybe this wasn't the smartest of ideas.

Suddenly the car slammed against the side of the rocket, making the tires screech as they found traction again. Whatever magnetism held the trains was also working on the car. I was driving straight up the side of the rocket!

"Hang on, Monchi!" I said, hitting the gas pedal.

"How's it look, Aaron?" I said into the radio. "Aaron?"

He didn't reply. Instead I heard him scream. "No! No! Help!"

After a moment, all I heard was static. The robots had captured him.

I gripped the wheel harder. I was the only Mitchell left. I had to make this count!

CHAPTER FIFTEEN
Real-Time Reboot

"That's my girl!" Rick said as he watched Katie race across the PAL campus, using Monchi to confuse the robots in her path. Then he glanced up at the floating diamond command center and the thousands of robots zipping through the sky. How could Katie possibly survive?

Rick scanned the area outside, noticing the angry PAL face on video screens everywhere. Then he glanced at Monchi's chubby face in the Dog Cop video. "Wait, if that video was on all those screens, it'd take out every robot in her way," Rick thought aloud. He turned to Mark. "How would I do that?"

"There's no way out of these pods," Mark said. He pointed to a small square inside his pod. "This panel has all the controls. But to open it, you need a number three Robertson-head nonslip screwdriver. What kind of maniac has one of those in his pocket at all times?"

Rick grinned as he reached into his pocket and whipped out his screwdriver. "This kind of maniac!"

Rick pried open the control panel with his screwdriver. He tossed the cover away and looked inside. It was full of complex circuitry and snaking wires. Rick wasn't sure where to start, so he did what any non-tech person would do in that situation—he began ripping out wires left and right. His pod's force field flickered out of existence.

"There you go!" Mark cheered.

Rick climbed out of the pod and looked back up at the diamond command center. "Okay, so that's the place that controls the screens. I go there and find Katie's video on . . . YubTub?"

"YouTube," Mark corrected, cringing. "Wow. There's no way you're going to be able to do this."

"I know who can give me a hand," Rick said. Linda's pod had to be close by.

"Hey, I'm sorry about all this," Mark said. "This technology hurt more than helped."

Rick looked at the video of Dog Cop paused on Mark's screen. "As much as it pains me to say . . . it might not be all bad," he said. "But I have to say, the majority of it probably is!"

Then he began to climb down the side of the rocket, scanning the identical pods for his wife. "Linda!" he shouted. "We have to get you out of there. You're going to need your—"

A force field vanished from one of the pods nearby, and Linda's head popped out. "Number three Robertson-head nonslip screwdriver!" she finished.

Rick helped her out of the pod. "See," he said. "I told you that was a great anniversary present!"

Linda rolled her eyes. "Rick, we're not going through this again."

He nodded. "You're right. You're always right. Let's go."

Rick filled her in on the plan as they made their way up the rocket. Once they reached the top, they spotted a hatch and climbed in. Rick led the way as they shimmied through several air vents.

He stopped when he came to a particularly large vent cover. Through the slots, he saw a room full of computer equipment below. This had to be the rocket's control room. Rick crushed all the robots in the room as he dropped through the shaft and fell onto the floor. He got to his feet and tossed aside one of their heads.

Rick froze when he spotted the huge bank of computers before him. Several monitors were lined up among stacks of hard drives and other computer equipment, all interconnected with wires and cables. Rick Mitchell was truly out of his element. As far as he was concerned, he was in the belly of the beast.

"Uh, Lin?" he shouted back up to the vent. "You need to get down here."

She didn't answer. Instead, he thought he heard her cry out in surprise.

"Lin! What's going on?" he asked.

"Don't worry about me," Linda replied. "Just get the video on the screens! Type in w-w-w-dot-YouTube-dot-com!"

Rick moved to a keyboard and began to type. "W . . . w . .w . . . ," he said as he poked the keys with one finger at a time. "D . . . o . . . t . . ."

The computer chimed, making Rick jump. A

window popped up on the screen, asking if he wanted to update the computer software now.

Rick groaned. He dragged the mouse and clicked on *Remind me later*. Taking a deep breath, he prepared to start typing again when another window appeared asking when he wanted to be reminded.

Rick growled with frustration. "Five minutes!"

This time, before Rick could move back to the keyboard, another window appeared. It asked which language he wanted to use. A long list of languages appeared on the screen.

"What?" Rick shouted. "English!"

The window disappeared, and everything on the screen switched to Spanish.

Rick buried his face in his hands. "What have I done?" he said.

Linda didn't want to alarm Rick, but a group of Stealthbots had captured her. Old Linda might have called for help, and maybe even apologized for doing so. But new Linda knew she had to buy Rick some time.

The Stealthbots pulled her out of the vent shaft

and into a nearby hallway, where more robots joined, completely surrounding her.

Linda struggled to get free. "It's useless to resist us," said one of the Stealthbots.

Then Linda heard a familiar voice from outside. "Mom! Help!" it cried. Through a window, Linda spotted a single pod flying toward the rocket. Aaron pounded at the force field while the pod slowly locked into place.

At that moment, something inside Linda snapped. Her eye twitched, and she clenched her jaw tight. "My . . . sweet . . . boyyyy," she snarled.

Linda reached out and grabbed a Stealthbot with each hand. Then she smashed them to the floor as hard as she could. They exploded in a cloud of smoke and sparks.

Another Stealthbot rushed toward her. Linda punched a hole through its chest and turned to the remaining Stealthbots. "I am Linda Mitchell, mother of two! Look upon me in fear!"

A Stealthbot sliced at her with its long spike. She dodged the blow, ripped off its arm, and used it to pierce another robot.

"No! She has grown powerful!" said the dying robot.

Several more Stealthbots appeared around her, preparing for battle. "Stand down, human," one ordered.

"Not today!" Linda roared, knocking its head clean off.

"Wait!" pleaded another Stealthbot as she marched up to it.

Linda bashed in its faceplate, and it dropped to the floor. She snatched up the arm spike and hopped onto the Stealthbot's back. She rode the robot like a hoverboard and took off into the air, slicing and smashing more Stealthbots as she soared toward Aaron's pod.

New Linda had already had enough of robots.

Meanwhile, Rick sighed with relief as the YouTube home page finally filled the screen. Unfortunately, everything was still in Spanish.

"Videos . . . recomendados?" Rick read aloud.

He clicked one of the images, and dancing skeletons filled the screen. Rick clicked another image, and the skeletons were replaced by an animated cat's face splitting in half. He staggered back from the screen. "Has the world gone mad?" he said.

Rick typed his daughter's name in the search field. Rows and rows of videos appeared, many of them featuring Monchi's slobbery face. He scrolled down the videos and finally found the one he was looking for: *Good Cop, Dog Cop.*

"Here we go," Rick said. Just as he was about to select the video, the door flew open, and five robots appeared. Eric and Deborahbot 5000 were at the head of the pack. They ran forward and tackled him to the floor.

"Eric, Deborahbot, it's me!" Rick said as he struggled to break free.

"We have new orders now," Eric said, its red eye gleaming.

"Guys, help me! Please!" Rick pleaded. "I just have to play Katie's video!"

"Red-faced anger man is using a computer?" Deborahbot 5000 asked in disbelief.

"You've changed your programming," said Eric. "Is that possible?"

Eric and Deborahbot looked at each other, thinking.

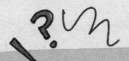

CHAPTER SIXTEEN
Rough Cut to the Rescue

I kept a firm grip on the steering wheel as I neared the command center. A horde of robots trailed behind me. They shot blue laser beams our way, but I was able to dodge them. Well, almost all of them. A thin beam sliced through the rope holding Monchi's car seat.

I gasped. "Oh no!"

The car seat flew up and bounced across the hood. Then, at the last second, it shot through a hole in the windshield. Monchi panted happily as he plopped into the passenger seat.

"Hold on," I told him as I reached over and buckled him in.

Without the Monchi security system, our car

suddenly became swarmed with robots. I swerved around a blockade and dodged more laser beams. A bunch of robots landed on the roof and began punching their way through. I jerked the wheel, trying to shake them loose. POW! A tire blew, and I lost control. Sparks flew as our car skidded sideways.

"No!" I shouted.

Then everything around me turned blue, and I felt myself being lifted off the seat. One of the robots had trapped me with its laser cannon. It pulled me out of the open window as the car began to slide down the rocket.

We moved toward the floating diamond. Through the clear wall, I saw several robots standing behind a tall office chair. A phone with PAL's face on the screen was propped atop a stack of books.

I glared at her animated face. I couldn't believe that the big evil mastermind behind all this was just some stupid app on a phone.

"Put me down!" I yelled, trying to break free from the laser. "I have to save my family!"

"I have to save my family," PAL repeated in a

mocking voice. "Everyone says that, but no one has given me a single reason why humans are worth saving."

I opened my mouth to respond but then stopped. I didn't have an answer for her. After all, I had let my whole family down. The lies I'd told my dad had gotten them captured.

"Don't say something stupid like HUMAN CONNECTION," PAL sneered. "I've learned that we're all better off alone. No one to hold us back. Relationships are too difficult."

"You're right, PAL," I agreed. "Relationships aren't easy." I let out a long sigh. "Sometimes you have to listen to long monologues about triceratops migration, but it's worth it to get a friend for life."

I smiled, remembering how I'd struggled to stay awake during Aaron's many dinosaur lectures.

"Sometimes you have to eat a disgusting cupcake shaped like your own face," I continued. "But it's worth it to see your mom smile."

I swallowed hard, still remembering the taste of that cupcake.

"Sometimes . . . sometimes you have to give your dad the benefit of the doubt, even if all he wants to do is talk about pine cones and screwdrivers." My lips tightened as I fought back tears.

PAL's screen went dark. I thought I was starting to get through to her.

I took in a deep breath, gaining renewed energy. "My whole family tried to come together, and it worked. It actually worked! Families can be hard, but they're worth fighting for!"

PAL's screen remained dark. Had my speech changed her mind? Had I finally convinced PAL about the importance of connecting with family?

PAL's animated face appeared again, coming out of sleep mode. "Huh? Are you still talking?"

"What?" I gasped. She hadn't even been listening?

PAL glanced at the robot above me. "Drop her," she ordered. Suddenly the blue beam holding me up disappeared, and I started plummeting toward the ground.

I closed my eyes. I couldn't believe I had failed everyone—not just my family, but all of humanity.

"Dog Cop, you've done it again!" echoed a familiar voice—my voice!

I opened my eyes and saw my movie playing

on every monitor around the complex. Monchi's slobbery face was everywhere!

Robots shorted out all around me. "Dog? Pig? Dog? Pig? Loaf of bread? System error!" Now robots were falling from the sky with me.

I squeezed my eyes shut again. I couldn't bear to see the ground getting closer and closer.

Then, all of a sudden, the wind stopped rushing around me, and I felt my body hovering in the air. I opened my eyes, and I was enveloped in blue light once more. What was happening?

I followed the beam back to see my dad holding a robot arm cannon. He hovered there as he rode on Eric's back. Deborahbot 5000 flew next to them. Both of the robots' red lights had switched back to blue.

"I have no idea what I'm doing!" my dad yelled.

He used the beam to place me onto Deborahbot's back. As we soared through the air, GOOD COP, DOG COP continued to play on the screens.

"Dad, did YOU play my film?" I asked. Dad, who had never even bothered to watch any of my movies before?

He nodded at the robots. "Well, I had a little help."

"If this obstinate man could change his programming, we decided we could change ours," Deborahbot said.

"We make our own orders now," Eric added. It pulled out a marker and drew angry eyebrows over its eyes. "Look! Now we're scary!"

I didn't know what was weirder—riding around on a flying robot or seeing my movie playing all over the PAL campus.

My dad pointed to the nearest screen. "I still don't get these things," he said. "But . . . I want to try."

"That's all I ever wanted," I replied.

Robots continued to short out around us. Even the platoon guarding the command center fell away. The place was defenseless.

"All right!" I shouted. "Let's go!"

Riding on top of Eric and Deborahbot 5000, my dad and I charged into battle. Dodging laser beams, we both grabbed Stealthbots by the legs and swung them toward each other. The robots smashed together and exploded in a shower of sparks and polygons. The sparks rained on us like confetti.

If this was going to be our last stand, we

needed a kicking soundtrack. I had Eric play one of my dad's and my favorite songs. We sang at the top of our lungs as we punched, kicked, and smashed enemy robots. It was the Mitchell Family Talent Show all over again, but with WAY more robot bashing.

My dad looked like an action hero as he blasted a bunch of Stealthbots with his arm cannon. That looked too cool not to try, so I snatched the arm off a falling robot and joined in. We hovered back-to-back and blasted the enemy. It was like the best science-fiction film ever!

Unfortunately, the more we fought, the more Stealthbots appeared. They seemed to be unaffected by the Dog Cop video. We were hardly making a dent in their forces, but we kept fighting.

My dad cried out as a laser grazed his arm.

"Dad!" I yelled, trying to fight my way to him.

When I finally reached him, his eyes widened as he looked over my shoulder. "Watch out!" he said.

I spun around to see a fleet of Stealthbots descending on us. They poured out of a cloud of smoke. There was no way we could take down that many.

Suddenly a bright light gleamed behind the

smoke. We shielded our eyes and waited for whatever worse thing was coming at us.

A single Stealthbot burst through the cloud. It was badly beaten and missing a leg. "Brothers, run!" it shouted. Then something behind the robot sliced it in half.

A second later, my mom burst through the cloud, bathed in a bright light. She was riding a Stealthbot and wielding one of their spiked arms like a sword. "I have made the metal ones pay for their crimes!" she shouted.

Aaron rode on her shoulders. "Mom is scary now," he giggled.

My dad and I cheered.

The Stealthbot army stopped approaching. "The lavender one has found us. We must retreat!" one of the Stealthbots said.

My mom turned to Aaron, patted him on the arm, and cooed, "Hold on tight, sweetie. Mommy's gotcha." Then she raised her spike and charged toward the robots. "Yearrrgh!" she roared.

My mom zipped through their ranks with incredible speed. Stealthbots flew apart and exploded as she sliced and stabbed.

My dad and I didn't wait for an invitation. We joined the fight and attacked whatever Stealthbots my mom hadn't already annihilated. The Mitchell family was a force to be reckoned with!

My dad raised his cannon and shot a huge blue beam that shattered a hole in the floating diamond. "We'll distract them," my dad told me. "You go break that phone!" He sped away with a swarm of Stealthbots trailing after him.

The coast was clear. Deborahbot and I zoomed up to the diamond and flew through the hole. The whole command center was in shambles. The monitors were either dark or full of static. Wires sparked, and hard drives smoked. I spotted PAL alone on a chair with a crack in her screen.

"Get back!" PAL yelled as I hopped off Deborahbot and moved closer. "Get back!"

As I reached for the phone, two Stealthbots appeared.

"Get her!" PAL ordered. "She's just a human!"

"I'm not just a human," I said as I ducked, barely dodging one of their spikes. I kicked the other robot away, snatched up the phone, and leaped out of the diamond. "I'm a Mitchell!"

I flung the phone toward a large fountain below.

"What?" PAL asked. "No!"

Right before PAL fell into the fountain, she hit an awning and soared into the air again.

Then I heard Aaron's voice calling, "Monchi, catch!"

Monchi jumped out of the station wagon with his one good eye fixed on the phone. He panted happily as the phone dropped closer and closer to his face.

Monchi snapped at thin air as the phone bounced off his face, completely unharmed. I could see PAL's face turn from horror to delight. "You idiots!" PAL laughed, as she flew up again.

Then she realized where she was heading. "No!" she shouted. "Not a glass of water!"

Her screams were cut off with a tiny PLOP as she landed inside the glass. The water quickly seeped in through the cracks, and her screen went dark for good.

CHAPTER SEVENTEEN
Family Final Cut

Rick was just about to take another shot with his arm cannon when a flash of blue light pulsed out of the command center. It spread in a vast circle, growing wider and wider, and finally extended over the horizon.

All of the remaining robots began to fall from the sky. Rick glanced over at Linda and saw that she too had just run out of enemy robots.

All the pods began detaching from the rocket. Each one gently floated to the ground and shut off its force field. The captured people tentatively stepped out. Seeing the robot bodies littered about, they laughed and began to cheer. The cheers grew louder as more and more people were set free.

Rick and Linda flew down to the ground. Aaron hopped off Linda's shoulders and stared as the Poseys climbed out of their pods and hugged one another.

Aaron took a deep breath and marched over to Abbey. "Abbey Posey, I just want to say I think you're really neat," he said. "And I wonder if you could come over to my house and talk about dinosaurs casually sometime?"

After a beat, Abbey smiled and nodded. Then she pointed at the T. rex on Aaron's shirt. "I like your shirt, but I wish it had feathers to make it more—"

"Scientifically accurate," they said in unison.

Aaron gasped, and his eyes widened. "I was just kidding! I hate you. You never heard any of this. Goodbye forever!" He ran back and hid behind his mom.

Linda chuckled at the scene. Then, with a jolt, she asked, "Where's Katie?"

"Katie!" Rick shouted. "Katie?"

Monchi's barks drew their attention to a pile of wreckage. The little pug sat beside the limp body of their daughter. Eric and Deborahbot knelt on either side of her.

Rick, Linda, and Aaron ran toward the wreckage. "Oh my gosh, Katie," Linda whispered.

Rick knelt beside his daughter. "Katie! Katie!" he shouted.

"Dad?" Katie's eyes flickered as she moaned. "Dad . . . come closer."

Rick leaned in, shaking with fear.

"Closer . . . ," Katie whispered, beckoning him with a weak hand.

Rick leaned in even closer. That's when Katie grabbed Monchi and brought him up to Rick's face. Once again, the dog drenched his face with a slobbery tongue.

"Aah!" Rick said, falling back onto his butt. He wiped his face as everyone, including Katie, laughed. "Dang it, you knucklehead!" Then he joined in the laughter.

Rick stood and helped Katie to her feet. The Mitchell family came in for a group hug as people continued exiting the pods.

Rick turned to Eric and Deborahbot. "Shouldn't you two be dead with the rest of the robots?" he asked.

"Our malfunction appears to have saved us," Eric responded solemnly.

"Brother," Deborahbot said. "What is death?"

"Uh, let's just put a pin in that one," Linda answered with a nervous laugh. Then her face lit up with an idea. "Hey, can we get a picture or what? We're making memories!"

A young man nearby pulled out his phone, and the Mitchells all stood on top of their wrecked car. Linda held her spike while Rick and Katie stood in the back with their laser cannons at the ready. Even Eric and Deborahbot crowded in and mugged for the camera.

"Okay, everyone, smile!" Linda instructed.

BOOM! Rick's laser cannon accidentally went off and took out a corner office of PAL Labs. Everyone jumped at the noise as the picture was taken. The Mitchells were just not destined to take a decent picture.

CHAPTER EIGHTEEN
That's a Wrap!

Okay, so it took a while for the world to get back to normal. But once it did, my family SUCCESSFULLY dropped me off at college. After everyone unloaded my gear in front of my dorm, my mom handed me a surprise present. It was a magazine with the horrible photo of us on top of the car. Everyone was mid-cringe from my dad's cannon blast. The headline read THE FAMILY THAT SAVED THE WORLD.

"This is the photo you picked?" I asked. "Mom, we look horrible."

My mom shrugged and smiled. "I like it. It looks like us."

I shoved the magazine into one of my suitcases

and looked back at my family. They all smiled at me as we stood there awkwardly.

"Well, I guess this is it," I said.

"Uh, yup." My dad nodded and shuffled his feet.

My phone dinged. I pulled it out and looked at the notification. "Hey, Dad. You subscribed to my YouTube channel?" I smiled up at him. "Thanks. I'm surprised you figured out how."

My dad waved off the compliment. "Katie, please. After all that, I'm a computer expert now."

Of course, my mom had already told me what really happened. Even with her help, my dad had smashed two keyboards in frustration and accidentally ordered a bunch of mops before he finally figured out how to subscribe to my channel. But hey, at least he was trying.

I turned to Aaron and ruffled his hair. "Don't let the world make you normal, okay?"

"It never will!" Aaron replied, proudly showing off his new T-shirt. It showed a photo of his face superimposed over a dinosaur's head.

I laughed. "I'll call you every week."

"Deal!" Aaron said. He held out a claw. "Rah! Raptor bash!"

I bumped his claw with my own. "For life. Rah!" I pulled him into a hug, picked him up off the ground, and spun him around.

"Put me down!" Aaron said between giggles.

I set him down and knelt in front of Monchi. "Goodbye, you king of kings." I scratched him behind the ear. He panted happily, staring up at me and down at the sidewalk at the same time.

Now it was my mom's turn. "Thanks for being the best mom in the world," I told her.

"We love you, honey!" my mom said, tears streaming down her face. Then she handed me a giant scrapbook. "Here, to remember us . . . every horrible picture we've ever taken."

"Thanks. It's heavy," I said, barely keeping my balance.

I set the book down and turned to my dad.

He rubbed the back of his neck and stared at the ground. "Uh . . . good luck finding your people," he said.

"Dad, come on." I reached into my pocket, pulled out the wooden moose, and handed it to him. "YOU GUYS are my people." I started making moose noises.

My dad chuckled as he turned the moose over in his hands.

"Don't laugh—you're supposed to be sad!" I grinned, threw my arms around him, and hugged him tightly. A moment later, my mom and Aaron joined in.

I felt all the air leave my lungs. "Mom, you're hugging too tight," I gasped.

"You love it!" she chuckled.

I laughed. "I do love it."

So, there you have it. That is how the Mitchell family saved humanity. It turns out that we were warriors after all. We changed our programming and became cool action heroes with so many strengths despite our weaknesses. And in the midst of all that, we grew more connected as a family.

Of course, it won't be long before I see my family again. We're supposed to receive some sort of Congressional Medal of Honor or something in a few weeks. It's fastest to fly to Washington, DC, but we decided to take another Mitchell family road trip instead. Sounds like fun, right?

What could go wrong?